"I love you, Brady," Marissa said.

"For heaven's sake, you only showed up on my doorstep two days ago. It's too soon for you to have any feelings for me. You don't even know me," he said.

"Yes, I do. I know you're kind and gentle—"

"Kind?" he asked roughly. "I'm a lot of things, Marissa, but kind is not one of them. And Lord knows I'm not gentle. I won't let you make me into a hero I'm not and then blame me later when I don't live up to the image."

"You could never disappoint me."

He stifled a groan. What sane man would push away a woman who looked at him as if he could hold back the tide?

"I want you, Brady."

His jaw tightened, and his words came out fiercely. "You don't know who you are. You don't know what wanting is."

"It's what I'm feeling. Heat and heaviness. Softness and fire."

"Stop it."

"It's you—"

His mouth came down on hers with all the pent-up desire in him. . . .

WHAT ARE *LOVESWEPT* ROMANCES?

They are stories of true romance and touching emotion. We believe those two very important ingredients are constants in our highly sensual and very believable stories in the *LOVESWEPT* line. Our goal is to give you, the reader, stories of consistently high quality that may sometimes make you laugh, sometimes make you cry, but are always fresh and creative and contain many delightful surprises within their pages.

Most romance fans read an enormous number of books. Those they truly love, they keep. Others may be traded with friends and soon forgotten. We hope that each *LOVESWEPT* romance will be a treasure—a "keeper." We will always try to publish

LOVE STORIES YOU'LL NEVER FORGET
BY AUTHORS YOU'LL ALWAYS REMEMBER

The Editors

LOVESWEPT® • 347

Fayrene Preston
Amethyst Mist

BANTAM BOOKS
NEW YORK • TORONTO • LONDON • SYDNEY • AUCKLAND

AMETHYST MIST

A Bantam Book / August 1989

If you would be interested in receiving protective vinyl
covers for your Loveswept books, please write to this address
for information:

Loveswept
Bantam Books
P.O. Box 985
Hicksville, NY 11802

ISBN 0-553-22017-9

Published simultaneously in the United States and Canada

PRINTED IN THE UNITED STATES OF AMERICA

O   0 9 8 7 6 5 4 3 2 1

One

The night and the storm conspired to blind and deafen her. She was exhausted and in pain, and she cried out as she stubbed her foot against something brutally hard. Instinctively she reached out. The rough bark of a tree scraped her palm.

She didn't know where she was. She couldn't think or see. She only knew it was imperative to keep moving.

Lightning punctured the darkness just before thunder exploded in a long loud burst. The sky seemed to be cracking open. A tree branch smacked her face and she staggered backward. Quickly she regained her footing and trudged on.

She was completely disoriented, but one thing was extremely clear to her: She couldn't let herself be trapped. No matter what, she had to free herself of the darkness and the storm.

She didn't see the light until she had nearly reached it.

The storm attacked the cabin. Inside, Brady McCulloch tossed another log on the fire, unaffected by the raging elements.

He settled his tall frame on the couch and reached for his coffee. Beside him a book lay open, waiting for him. In the stone fireplace, the flames flared and danced, giving off hisses, sparks, and heat.

The intensity and violence of storms had always pleased Brady. They combined beauty and passion with the great ability to destroy. To his way of thinking, storms imaged life.

Thunder rolled across the heavens with ever-increasing strength until it broke apart with a sound and a force that shook the cabin's windows. Brady didn't flinch, just as he didn't flinch at life. Not anymore.

He crossed his long legs at the ankles and sipped his coffee. According to the weatherman, this storm front was huge and would linger over the area for quite some time. It would be good for his work, he thought with satisfaction. Somehow it seemed natural to him to create something beautiful and alive in an electrically charged atmosphere.

At his feet, Rodin, his Irish setter, abruptly lifted his head and looked toward the door.

"What is it, boy?"

Rodin spared Brady a fleeting glance before

riveting his curious gaze once more on the front door.

Brady gave a low chuckle. "You love company, don't you? I hate to be the one to break it to you, but you sure picked the wrong person to live with."

Apparently unperturbed by his master's view of his life, Rodin rose and trotted to the big pine door. He sniffed at its base for a minute, then raised his head in Brady's direction with brown eyes full of supplication.

"I'm telling you, no one's going to come see us tonight."

Rodin stared unblinkingly.

Brady sighed. "You're not going to be happy until I open the door, are you?"

Rodin's tail wagged eagerly back and forth.

"Okay, boy, you win." Brady set aside the mug and got to his feet. He didn't put himself out very often, he reflected with amusement. But Rodin provided undemanding company and affection and in return asked for very little. To Brady's mind, that made the dog an exception to the rule.

He unbolted the lock and pulled open the door.

Lightning hurtled out of the sky and struck the top of a not-too-distant pine tree, splitting it apart.

And a woman fell into his arms.

"What the hell?"

After the first dumbfounded moment passed, his instincts took over. He half-carried, half-dragged her into the cabin, laid her on the floor, and pushed the door closed against the storm. Then he turned back and surveyed his unexpected guest.

From the top of her dark head to the bottom of her booted feet, she was soaking wet. The large swelling above her left eye reached all the way to her hairline and was turning purple. Surface cuts ribboned her face.

Rodin, eager to greet the new arrival, was sniffing around her neck and hair.

"Sit, Rodin." Brady knelt beside the woman and felt her wrist for a pulse. He found it strong, though slightly erratic.

Giving a brief prayer of thanks, he carefully raised her upper body and removed her raincoat, one arm at a time. A cream-colored silk blouse and linen trousers were plastered to a fine-boned, elegantly formed figure. He lay her back down and quickly ran his hands over her legs and arms. She'd obviously been in some sort of accident. But his fear that she had broken bones was unfounded. Shock was the next thing he considered; she needed to be warm and dry.

With an easy strength, he scooped her into his arms and carried her upstairs to his bedroom, where he stripped off her clothes. After a brief hesitation at the lacy scraps of underwear, he skimmed them off with a minimum amount of effort.

Her skin was white and translucent and fleetingly inspired him to wonder what it would be like to work with alabaster. But her skin was also cold, and he quickly tucked her beneath the covers.

She felt his hands on her body as he took the cold, wet, heavy clothes from her. He had strong, powerful hands, and his sure touch caused her no alarm. Relief flooded through her when the last remaining article of clothing disappeared from her sore and hurting body.

She heard the storm, but its wrath no longer hammered at her. The pain still stabbed through her head, but it was not uppermost in her mind. *He* was. With great force of will, she opened her eyes and stared up at the arrogant, hard lines of the face above her. And what she saw reassured her. It was as if someone had ridged, grooved, and folded a sheet of bronze into the unyielding angles and creases of his face. And when he fastened his eyes on her, she saw that they had been created from cold gray steel.

He would hold back the storm and keep her safe.

Her eyes caught Brady off guard. They were lovely, the color of amethyst, and the utter trust they contained shocked him. As did her words.

"Thank God I found you," she whispered.

A softness he hadn't been aware he still possessed moved inside him. He sat down on the bed beside her and adjusted the covers over her. "Were you looking for me?"

"Oh, yes."

Memories flashed in his head, and the softness disappeared. "Okay, you found me. Now what?"

She gave him a hint of a smile.

The uncomplicated sweetness of her smile irritated him, even while he acknowledged the irrationality of his feeling. But it had been a long time since anyone had been able to visit him without his consent. "How did you find me?"

Her brow creased with brief confusion even as her eyes registered the pain of the gesture.

"Never mind. It doesn't matter," he said. "You've gone to a hell of a lot of trouble for nothing."

"I have?"

He nodded curtly. "As soon as possible, you're going back to wherever it is you came from."

"Oh." Her voice showed complete acceptance.

"What happened anyway? Did you lose control of your car in the storm?"

"Storm," she agreed on a whispered breath. "But I'm safe now."

Her lids fluttered closed, and he was left frustrated. Dammit, she seemed so fragile. How badly was she hurt, he wondered, then gave a low curse at himself. He could speculate from now until next week, and he still wouldn't be helping her.

The movement of the mattress as he rose brought her back to full wakefulness, and she panicked. Flinging out a hand, she managed to catch his shirt sleeve. "You're not going to leave me, are you?"

The fear in her eyes overrode everything else he was feeling. He placed his hand over hers with a compassion that was not usual to him. "I was just going to get a few things for you."

"Things?"

"Something to clean your face, some towels so that I can dry you, and something for you to wear."

"Oh." She fought against the heaviness of her lids. "My head hurts."

"I'm sure it must. I'll bring an ice pack too. It will help with the swelling and the pain. I don't think I should give you anything for pain just yet though."

She accepted his judgment without question. "Whatever you say." Just before her thick dark lashes touched her cheeks, she murmured, "You won't be gone long, will you?"

"No, I won't."

Despite his promise, he stood rooted to the spot, staring down at her. Damn! Something about her was bothering him. What was it? He had deliberately kept himself isolated these past fifteen years and, as a result, hadn't been faced with a problem he couldn't solve. And, of course, never before had a woman fallen out of a storm and into his arms. A woman with amethyst-colored eyes.

Oh, hell. His disturbed senses could be traced to the fact that she was injured and needed medical attention. It was as simple as that. He only wished helping her was going to be equally simple.

Under normal circumstances he would put her into his four-wheel-drive Jeep and take her down the mountain to the hospital. But there was only one bridge spanning the river and leading onto the road down the mountain, and the storm had undoubtedly washed out that bridge. He wouldn't be surprised if the woman's accident had occurred because of the bridge . . . or the flooded road.

Lord, she was beautiful, he thought, annoyed that she was having such an effect on him. Take away the scratches, and her skin would be flawless; take away the pallor that was natural in her injured condition, and her milk-white skin would glow. And he had never before seen eyes so like amethysts.

He stopped. Had she sought him out? If so, why? Over the years the number of people who had tried to invade his privacy, wanting bits and pieces of him for their own personal gain or satisfaction, had gradually diminished. So why now? Why her? What did she want from him? If she hadn't sought him out, then why had she thanked God for *finding* him?

Her sudden moan of pain drove the questions from his mind and sent him striding across the room and down the stairs.

He was gone only minutes, but when he returned she was awake again, her hands worrying the edge of the quilt. As he carried a tray to the bedside table, her extraordinary eyes followed him.

"I'm so glad you're back," she said softly.

"Are you?"

She nodded, then winced.

"Better be still. If you need moving, I'll do it." He reached for a cloth, dipped it into the bowl of warm water, wrung it out, then brought it to her face. "I'll try to be as gentle as possible," he said, then cursed as he heard her whimper. "I'm sorry, but I have to do this."

"It's all right," she whispered.

"Don't try to be brave," he said, using a biting tone as an unconscious defense against the effect her pain had on him.

She grimaced as his sharp words beat hurtfully against her eardrums and skull.

Taking up a towel, he carefully rubbed the moisture from the long black strands of her hair. Black azure, he thought absently, then caught himself. But he had seen her grimace and softened his voice. "I want you completely dry so that there's no possibility of your getting chilled. As soon as they repair the bridge, you're leaving."

"Bridge?" She frowned.

"The old wooden bridge you had to drive over to get here. Every time we have any kind of storm, the river rises and the bridge is washed out." He flung the towel aside, pushed off the bed, and went to his closet in search of one of his oldest, softest flannel shirts. "Is that what happened to you? Did you get caught on the bridge?" He found a blue and black plaid shirt and turned back only to discover that her eyes were closed again. "If that is what happened," he said, talking to himself now, "then you're damned lucky to be alive. In fact, it would have been a feat for anyone on this mountain out in that storm to stay alive."

He shook his head with disgust at himself and returned to her side. He had the shirt on her and was doing up the buttons when she

opened her eyes again. The impact of her amethyst gaze made his fingers clumsy. He found
himself fumbling with one of the middle buttons, and the edge of his hand brushed against
the soft mound of her breast beneath the flannel.

She waited calmly and without any sign of
embarrassment until he conquered the button
and moved on to the next. She didn't seem to
mind that a complete stranger had undressed
her and was now dressing her, he thought,
slightly vexed, then reminded himself that she
had had little choice.

"How many dogs do you have?" she asked.

He glanced over his shoulder at Rodin. The
Irish setter watched with interest from a corner
of the fireplace, the one place in the room besides the bed itself that gave him an uninter-
rupted view of her. "How many do you see?"

"One. Well, one and a half actually."

"Double vision," he muttered.

"But I see only one of you." She studied him.
"You have a very hard face."

The shirt safely buttoned, he brought the covers back over her. "I'm surprised you can even
think. From the size of that lump, I'd say you're
in a hell of a lot of pain."

"I am." She spoke without emotion. "What's
your dog's name?"

"Rodin." He gently laid the ice pack on her
forehead. "We'll talk tomorrow when you're feeling better. For now, I have to get you through
the night."

"You can do it." She curled her fingers around
his wrist. "I'm so glad I found you."

"Yeah, you said that."

He started to rise, but her eyes widened with alarm and her grip tightened with surprising strength.

"May I ask you a question?"

He nodded, cautious. He didn't like personal questions, especially when he didn't know what the questioner would do with the information.

"Who am I?"

Two

The storm roared overhead. Brady stared at her, stunned. "What did you say?"

"Who am I?"

"Don't you know?"

"No."

"Amnesia?" His tone was incredulous. "You're kidding."

"I don't know who I am."

The fear in her voice matched the panic in her eyes, and in the face of it, he tasted the unfamiliar bitterness of helplessness. "Great, just great."

"I'm sorry." She dropped her hand from his wrist.

"Why didn't you tell me sooner?"

"I—I only realized . . ."

"Do you know where you are?"

"No." Her breaking voice divided the word into two syllables.

"You're in Arkansas. In the Ozarks, about forty miles from Samsonville."

"Oh."

"Does that ring a bell?"

"No." She didn't seem to notice her ragged, torn nails as she pleated and unpleated the top edge of the quilt.

"Can you remember anything about your accident, anything at all?"

"I'm sorry. I really am."

He stared broodingly at her pale, beautiful face and thought of how much she must have gone through to reach him. Using his fingers as a comb, he absently untangled several strands of the dark hair that lay over the white pillow. "It's nothing to worry about. I've heard that amnesia can sometimes happen when a person receives a blow to the head, but it's only temporary."

"Really?"

Her panic eased and was replaced by faith and confidence in him. She was looking at him as if he were Superman, he thought, disturbed. Unable to hold her gaze, he turned away and began rearranging the items on the tray. "Yes, really. By morning, I'm sure you'll have remembered everything."

"That's good."

The long silence from her that followed eventually drew his gaze back to her. "What's wrong?"

"There's this terrible blankness in my mind. It's . . . frightening."

He sighed, finding himself torn. For one brief moment he wished for the ability to be as wonderful as she obviously thought he was, so that he could make everything right for her. But the wish was absurdly out of character for him and the moment passed. "I can understand your fear, but try to look at it this way—there are a lot of people who would give anything if they could forget their pasts."

"Are you one of those people?"

He grinned at the idea. His past had been the lesson that had changed his life for the better, and it wasn't something he wanted to forget. "No."

Immediately she was repentant. "It was a silly question, wasn't it? You're a man who could deal with anything."

"Do you usually form opinions of people so quickly?" This woman was making him aware that there were things he might not be able to handle—namely making her better. It wasn't a good feeling.

"Yes. No. I don't know."

He allowed a slight smile to indent the severe brackets around his mouth, an effort to ease her unrest. "That was certainly a multifaceted answer. I'm impressed." He reached up to adjust the ice pack on her head. "Is this helping with the pain?"

"I suppose. I don't know. It just hurts."

"I'm sure it does," he murmured. "Why don't you shut your eyes." Those eyes that could haunt a dead man. "Try to sleep."

"Yes, all right. You'll be here, won't you?"

"I'll be nearby." Somehow he couldn't see himself getting much sleep tonight. "If you need anything, just call out."

Her lashes almost reached her cheeks, when they flew up again. "What should I call you?"

He looked at her blankly. "Call me?"

"What's your name?"

"Oh. Brady. Brady McCulloch."

A smile curved her lips, unconsciously provocative, and her eyes slowly closed. "Brady," she whispered.

He put a match to the kindling beneath the logs in the bedroom fireplace and waited until it caught. He carefully secured the fire screen, made sure she was resting, and went downstairs.

Rodin gazed plaintively at his master but remained on the floor beside the bed.

After adding a log to the living room fire, Brady turned his attention to the soggy raincoat on the floor by the front door. He hadn't discovered any sort of identification in her other clothing, but in the right-hand pocket of the raincoat he found a gas credit card imprinted with the name Marissa Berryman. Somewhere she must have stopped for gas and forgotten to replace the card in her purse.

Marissa. He tilted back his head and stared at the ceiling, and as if the pine were transparent, her pale lovely image sprang vividly to mind. Too vividly.

A rumble of thunder sounded in the distance. *What a hell of a night,* he thought, and headed for the spare room and the radio.

He settled in front of the CB and called the local chief of police. "Tom, this is Brady McCulloch. Come in. Over."

He adjusted the volume as he heard Tom Harris's easy, good-humored voice ask, "So, how are things at the top of the mountain? Over."

"Wet. Over."

"Same down here, And the forecast is for lots more wet. Guess we'll have to cancel tomorrow evening's poker game. Too bad. I had big plans for your money. Over."

Brady gave a short laugh. "Keep dreaming. There's no harm. Over."

"That's the way I feel about it too. Anything I can do for you besides letting you keep your money a few days longer? Over."

"As a matter of fact, there is. The storm sent me an uninvited guest. She's been in some sort of accident and has suffered a blow to the head. To top it off, she can't remember who she is or what happened to her. Over."

Tom gave a low whistle. "Damn. We can't airlift her to the hospital in this weather, but I can patch you through to a doctor at the hospital. Over."

"That's what I was hoping. I know rudimentary first aid, and she's resting now, but I'd feel better if I could talk to a doctor." He paused, then wondered at his hesitation in telling Tom her name. "I found a gas credit card in her pocket. Has the name Marissa Berryman on it. Can you trace it? Over."

"I can try. Credit card companies aren't obliged to cooperate. Sometimes they'll help, sometimes they demand a court order. Just depends on the company. If they do demand a court order, we could be in trouble. Judge Reiser has taken his missus off on a vacation, you know. But we may get lucky. Just remember, if they decide to help, all you can expect is a billing address. Over."

"I understand. Over."

"Okay, give me the information. Over."

Brady reeled off the spelling of her name, the name of the company, and the credit card number. "When do you think you can get back to me? Over."

"It's Friday night, so Monday is the best I can do. I have to wait for the next business day. In the meantime, I'll patch you through to the hospital."

She'd been asleep for about an hour when the storm broke with renewed fury over the cabin. Through the peals of thunder her screams reached him, cutting across his nerves like a sharp knife. He raced upstairs to find Rodin standing with anxious gaze fixed on the woman in the bed.

Her eyes were squeezed shut, and tears slid from beneath the bunched eyelashes. He sat down beside her and gripped her arms. "What's wrong, Marissa?" A sob escaped her lips. "Marissa, open your eyes and look at me. I need you to tell me if your pain is worse. Marissa?"

Her eyes opened to reveal confusion and desperation as they focused on him. "Oh, Brady, thank God." She struggled to sit up, but before he could reach out to help her, she grabbed her head and moaned in agony.

"Don't *do* that." He pulled her roughly into his arms, though fully aware of the care he needed to use in handling her. He felt strangely compelled to pull her against him, as if his body might somehow transfer its strength to hers. Madness. He had never comforted anyone in his life and had no idea where this impulse had come from.

She rested against him, shuddering with relief. His touch soothed her pain. His arms provided consolation and warmth. His strength allayed her fears. A breath came out as a soft sigh.

He rubbed her back, the pressure of his hand light and easy. "What were you trying to do, jerking up like that?"

"This."

"This?"

"I wanted you to hold me," she said softly.

"Just ask next time, okay? Don't jerk up like that." His hand went to the back of her head, his fingers spreading through the still-damp hair to cradle her head. "Is the pain very bad?"

"It's . . . bad."

He tensed, angry that he could do so little to help her. "There's some Tylenol around here someplace. I wish I had something stronger, but the doctor said it was best that you stick with the mild stuff anyway."

"Doctor?"

"Yeah, I spoke with a resident at the local hospital." He made a motion to release her. "I'll be back in a minute with the pills."

"No!" She clutched at him.

"Easy now. The doctor said you should stay quiet."

"I will. I will. I promise. Please, just stay here and hold me."

"Okay. For a little while." Holding her was incredibly easy, he thought. He gazed down at the top of her head. "What happened? Why the scream?"

"I was having a nightmare. I was outside. I was alone again. Trapped inside—"

"Shhh, it's all right. The storm sounds like hell, but it's not going to touch you. I built this house myself, and it can withstand a hell of a lot more than Mother Nature's throwing at us now. I guarantee it."

"I knew you'd keep me safe," she murmured, the side of her mouth moving against his chest as she spoke.

She was nothing more than a frightened, hurt child, he told himself, and she needed comforting. The problem was she felt like a woman to him and with little effort he could respond like a man. With a knuckle beneath her chin, he tilted her head back so that he could see her face. Then he wished he hadn't. Even bruised and cut, she could fascinate him if he let her. "I have some good news."

"What?" she asked softly.

"I know your name. It's Marissa Berryman."

It seemed to him that she stopped breathing for a moment. "How do you know that?"

"I found a gas credit card in the pocket of your raincoat."

"And you think it's mine?"

"Stands to reason. Who else could it belong to?" He paused. "Does the name sound familiar at all?"

Large crystal tears formed in her eyes. "No. No, it doesn't. Not at all. Why can't I—"

"Don't get upset. I told you that you'll remember, and you will." He brushed his hand tenderly over her cheek then brought her head back to his chest. After a time, he felt her relax against him, but when her silence lengthened, he became worried. "Marissa?"

She listened to the sound of the name that he had said was hers. It was rather pretty, she decided, and tried to imagine what kind of person would have such a name. Then thinking became too much of an ordeal, and she blanked her consciousness of everything but the blissful security of the arms holding her fast.

"Marissa?"

She drew a deep, shaky breath. "Could you . . . could you please stay with me for the rest of the night?"

"Sure. I'll sit over by the fire with Rodin until you get back to sleep." Slowly he lowered her back to the pillows, but her fingers clutched at the front of his shirt.

"No, you need to stay here in bed with me and hold me. Please."

"Marissa, I—"

"*Please,* I won't be any bother. I promise."

"You don't know—" The growing desperation he saw in her eyes stopped his objection. A frightened, hurt child, he reminded himself. "All right, all right." He gently loosened her fingers from his shirt. "I guess it won't do any harm. At least this way I won't have to try to stay awake to listen for you, and maybe we can both get some rest."

She stared up at him, trusting, pale, bruised, and very beautiful. He almost changed his mind about the wisdom of spending the night in bed with her, holding her, but then he saw the energy it was taking for her to fight the pain.

"I'll be right back."

"Oh, no, wait." Her eyes widened in panic. "Where are you going?"

"Just into the next room." He jerked his head toward the bathroom door. "That's where the Tylenol is. It won't take me a minute."

The apprehension that clouded her eyes made him curse silently, but he hurried and was soon back. He gave her the pills, built up the fire, slid onto the bed beside her, and gathered her close.

The next morning, solid sheets of rain were still pouring out of the heavens, but the wind had died down from a bluster to a whine, and the thunder and lightning had passed. From her position on the downstairs couch, Marissa eyed Brady from beneath thick, dark lashes.

"Let me know if you get cold," he said absently, standing in front of the fire with one hand braced against the mantle and one booted foot propped on the raised hearth.

"I will," she said, wishing he would look at her. He seemed very remote, but she wasn't really bothered. She remembered how he had cradled her aching head against his strong chest through the night. Every so often when she'd heard his voice speaking to her, she had answered, and it had seemed to make him happy.

The other thing she remembered was the surprising reassurance she had drawn from his hard face and cold gray eyes. But now she realized she hadn't noted anything else about his appearance. She had no idea what he had been wearing. Today, though, a navy-blue sweater that looked as though it was hand-knitted stretched across his broad shoulders and a pair of well-washed jeans revealed tight buttocks and muscular thighs and calves. Looking at him, she experienced a curious flutter in her stomach. Her throbbing pain and fear last night must have been blinding, she concluded, for her not to realize what a ruggedly attractive man he was.

Impulsively she said, "You're a very sexy man."

His head whipped around. "What?"

"I said—"

He gave a curt wave of his hand. "Never mind. Just tell me why you said that. Who are you judging me by?"

She was confused by his reaction. "Judging you?"

Impatience surged through him at having to

explain. "What point of reference are you using to come to that conclusion?"

She shrugged, uncomfortable. "I don't know. I was just thinking about you and . . ."

He took a few steps toward her, intense and strangely driven. "Come on, Marissa. What other man do you consider sexy?"

She looked at him, disquiet gathering in her eyes. "No one."

"How can you be so sure? Have you remembered anything?"

She felt immediately better as she realized what his questions were about. He was concerned with her memory. "When and if I do, I'll tell you, Brady. I'm not keeping anything from you."

"I know that." He dropped heavily into the big rocking chair by the fireplace. Lord, what was wrong with him? His reaction to her comment had come up out of nowhere, making him momentarily forget the amnesia that had made her as ingenuous, as guileless as a child. "I'm sorry, Marissa. I was wrong to badger you like that."

"You don't have to apologize. I know you're concerned about me."

"Yes, well, what's important is that you're better this morning," he said firmly. "Your skin has more color, and you told me your pain is less."

"I do have less pain, but—"

"That's good, that's good. And what you're going through with this amnesia is natural. You not only had the blow to your head, but you had the trauma of whatever happened to you during the storm."

She lapsed into contemplative silence, allowing him a chance to study her. His big shirt almost swallowed her, the sleeves rolled up in thick layers to just below her elbow, the collar standing away from her slender white neck. A blanket covered her bare legs. Her long hair laid in dark swirls around her shoulders.

"It seems strange that I don't recognize my own name," she said after awhile. "I mean, I guess it's a nice name. But I don't get any feeling about the name one way or the other."

"It will come, I promise."

Gravely she looked at him. "Nothing is familiar, Brady. It's as if I never existed. There's only you and the storm in my mind."

He bolted to his feet, walked to the window, leaned his shoulder against the wall, and gazed unseeingly out at the rain.

She was much too honest and trusting for her own good, he thought. And too direct for his peace of mind. And too beautiful. Her memory couldn't return soon enough for him.

The rainstorm would come and go for another few days so the bridge couldn't be restored, and she would have to stay here. Damn, but he wanted her gone.

He hated the interruption to his work.

He hated the invasion of his privacy.

He hated the pain she was enduring.

Marissa watched Brady. He was her world, all she knew. She could cope with the pain and the loss of her memory as long as he stayed near her. It was strange, but as soon as she had opened her eyes and looked at him, she had known she could trust and depend on him. She was not at all troubled by the idea of being stranded here with him. But she could tell *he* was troubled.

"What's wrong, Brady? What's bothering you?"

"I was just wishing the damn bridge wasn't out."

"What good would it do if it could still be used? I can't remember where my home is."

"Or who's there waiting for you? Aren't you concerned that someone might be worried about you?"

As she thought about it, an uneasiness stole over her. "No, no, I'm not. I guess I should be, though."

"Do you *think* there is someone?"

"I've told you over and over again, I don't know." She rubbed at a spot on her forehead that wasn't swollen.

An answer, even if she knew it, wouldn't change anything, he thought moodily. Within a few days she would be gone. A few more days and she would be out of his thoughts entirely. He should just leave the matter alone. "You're not wearing a wedding ring."

"I'm not?" She jerked her hand down to examine it and saw slender well-shaped fingers that bore no rings. For some reason she felt a rising panic. "I—I'm not."

"There's no indentation where a ring might have been, either."

"You're right," she said, her gaze darting to

him, then back to her left hand. "That means I couldn't be married, doesn't it?"

"Probably."

"That's what it means," she said quickly. "I'm not married, and I think we ought to stop talking about it. It's useless to speculate anyway, but I am not married. I know I'm not."

His eyes narrowed. The rate of her breathing had increased, her voice had turned unsteady. Thinking of herself as married definitely disturbed her. "What makes you think you're not married, Marissa?"

"Because . . ." Her fingers folded inward into a fist, and she stared with horrified fascination at the ring finger of her clenched hand. "Just because. Anyway, it's not important. I'm fine as I am, right here. I don't need my memory back."

"What do you mean, you're fine as you are? Don't you want to remember?"

"Of course . . . of course, I do."

"You said you didn't."

"It's just that you're taking good care of me. I'm safe and warm. My double vision has disappeared. I still have a headache but—"

"No buts. You're experiencing nausea, a classic symptom of concussion."

"At least I'm not throwing up. And that broth you gave me earlier tasted wonderful." She dropped her hand over the side of the couch and patted Rodin's head.

She didn't want to remember! The realization came to Brady with great certainty. And his constant questions were only making her agitated, when she needed to rest.

But why didn't she want to remember? Could she be running away from someone—or something? If so, why?

She wasn't keeping anything from him. He doubted she was capable of a lie. When she'd lost her memory, she apparently also lost all of the normal guards and defenses people develop as they grow older and learn to function in a world that is not always kind.

It was the *unconscious* level of her mind about which he was curious. For the first time he was aware that the cause of her amnesia could be emotional as well as physical. He had to be careful, stifle his curiosity, wait. He had to allow her to remember in her own time. And he had to protect her from her fears . . . and from *him* . . . because as long as her memory remained buried, she was as vulnerable as a baby.

She fidgeted with the ice pack on her head, unsure whether it was really helping her heal or simply numbing her scalp so that she couldn't feel anything. She hadn't seen her face last night, but Brady had said she looked slightly better than she had last night. She reached again for the mirror she had asked him to bring her a short time ago and held it up to her face, searching urgently for some sign of familiarity. There was none.

"That's the third time you've looked at yourself in the mirror. Aren't you happy with what you see?"

She relaxed, hearing the dry humor in his voice. "I guess it's a nice enough face, or at least it will be when this lump goes down and these scratches heal." She gingerly touched her cheek, feeling nothing but detachment about the woman in the mirror. "It's like I'm looking at a photograph of a stranger."

"Trust me, it's no photograph. That's you, and there are women who would pay thousands of dollars to look like you. Even with a lump on the head."

"I do, you know."

"What?"

"Trust you."

He straightened up, away from the wall. "It was a figure of speech. What can I get you? Another cup of broth?"

She didn't want him to leave her yet, even though he'd be close by in the kitchen. She said the first thing that came into her mind. "What do you do here? I mean, do you do some kind of work?"

"Yeah, I do some kind of work."

"Where? Do you have an office you go to in Samsonville?"

He knew that her ignorance of what he did was as genuine as his reluctance to tell her about it was instinctive. "I have a shop out back."

"Shop?" She frowned over the word.

"Workshop. Studio. I . . . work with wood. Or at least for the moment, I do."

The frown cleared. "Oh, you mean you make cabinets and furniture and stuff like that?"

A smile surfaced. "Yeah, stuff like that."

"You have a nice smile. You should smile more often."

He jammed his hands forcefully into the pockets of his jeans. "Marissa, do you want more broth?"

She accepted his impatience as easily as she had accepted his smile. "That would be nice."

Three

The day stretched endlessly for Brady. Marissa seemed to be everywhere. He was encircled by the softness of her voice, the sweetness of her smile, the adoration in her eyes—everything about her seemed to fill the corners of his house and reach to the rafters. Amazing, really, when he considered she had left the couch only a few times.

Marissa was getting to him.

The way she looked at him worked on his mind, just as how she looked worked on his body. She was giving all of herself to him. It required all in return, and that was a responsibility he didn't want.

He had never known himself to feel so restless and fidgety. By day's end, he actually considered taking a ten-mile jog through the rain-soaked forest. But what he had done instead was suggest to Marissa that she might like to take a shower.

Now he was calling himself all kinds of fool as he adjusted the spray of water until the temperature was just right. He turned, shaking the excess moisture from his forearm. "Are you sure you can manage?"

"I think so," she said, gazing around the bathroom. Slats of cedar formed geometric patterns. Colorful gold-and-green-flecked tiles lined a shower that was big enough for two. The effect was striking and masculine, like Brady, she thought. "This was a marvelous idea. Thank you for thinking of it. The hot water will help my sore muscles."

He frowned uncertainly. "I just wish I had a tub. You're not too steady on your feet."

"I'm sure I'll be able to manage."

"Okay, then. There are the towels." He pointed toward a stack of thick forest-green towels. "Everything else you need should be in the shower."

"Shampoo?"

"Yeah. It's not anything fancy, but it should get your hair clean."

She grimaced. "My hair feels really grubby."

"It looks wonderful," he said, then could have bitten his tongue. "I'm going to leave the door cracked, so call out if you need anything. I'll be in the next room."

She smiled at him. "Thank you."

His mind told him to walk out the door; his body swayed toward her. Fortunately, his confusion lasted only a moment. He left, careful to leave the door ajar.

She slipped off his shirt and her underpants and stepped into the heavenly hot water, sighing with pleasure. The spray nozzle had been set to gentle. Brady, she thought. It seemed to irritate him when she said nice things about him, but this was just another indication of how thoughtful he was. To her mind he was a remarkable man. He . . .

A wave of dizziness swept over her. "Brady!" Her hand shot out to the wall to brace herself.

The bathroom door immediately flew open. "What's wrong?"

"I guess I'm not as strong as I thought."

"That's what I was afraid of." He was across the room with his hand on the shower-door handle before he was able to stop himself. Anxious about her, yet indecisive about what he should do, he stood there. "Are you nearly finished?"

"I haven't even started."

"Then, I'd better wait in here with you. You could fall. Anything could happen to you." He retreated to the other side of the room. "I'll be over here."

With a smile to herself, she reached for the soap. Even though she could only hear Brady's voice, his nearness made her feel safe. Today, as her pain had slowly receded and her strength had gradually returned, she had begun to think about her life before the accident. She didn't want to think about it. She wanted only Brady—his kindness, his caring, his strength.

She couldn't remember the bridge, but it appeared she must have somehow got across the river and then climbed the rest of the way up the mountain to reach Brady. Her old life lay somewhere on the other side of that bridge. As far as she was concerned, it could remain there. But Brady seemed convinced she would eventually remember, so she had to consider the possibility. And she had. But since there was no sign that she had worn a wedding ring in the recent past, there was no real reason why she couldn't stay with Brady. *If* he wanted her to stay . . .

Brady leaned his hips against the sink and scowled at the shower door. Through the frosted glass he could see the slim, curving silhouette of Marissa's body.

She stroked the soap up and down her body, and he hungrily followed her every movement. When she turned sideways to him, her back to the shower spray, he was able to see the alluring outline of her beautifully shaped breasts and their rigid tips. Totally unaware of what she was doing, she was seducing him.

He was hard and burning. The hot steam from the shower swirled out, surrounding him with a soft warm mist, but he knew that wasn't the reason his forehead was beaded with sweat.

"This spray on my shoulders feels wonderful," she called. "I don't know why they're so sore."

"Probably because you tensed at the time of the accident."

"I guess so," she said vaguely, not particularly wanting to think about the accident.

He wiped his forehead with the back of his

arm. "Why don't you wind it up in there? This is the first time you've been up for any length of time."

She laid the soap on the ledge. "Let me just wash my hair. . . ."

She backed under the spray, raised her hands to her head, and cried out.

Brady came away from the sink, his muscles taut, ready for action. "What happened?"

"The muscles in my shoulder are too sore for me to raise my arms that high."

She sounded so upset, he spoke before he thought. "I'll wash your hair."

"You will?"

He closed his eyes. *Damn.* "Yes. Just get out, dry off, and I'll go set things up in the kitchen. Take all the time you need to rest, then come down when you're ready." He heard the water turn off and hesitated. "Do you need anything?"

"Could you hand me a towel?"

She opened the door and reached a long slender arm out to him, inadvertently exposing a tantalizing portion of firm white breast and a tight pink bud. He thrust the towel at her and hurriedly left the room with a muttered curse.

Downstairs minutes later he was still cursing. What a hell of a situation. In the course of fifteen years he'd had women here. They'd made him feel good. Marissa made him feel like a simmering volcano.

Without even trying, she was tying him in knots. Lord help him, what would it be like for him if she *tried*?

One thing at a time, he cautioned himself.

Help her as much as you can, be patient until she regains her memory, then send her on her way.

Right.

He picked up a dishtowel and hurled it across the room just as Marissa walked into the kitchen.

He didn't even try to explain. "I hope leaning over the sink is not going to bother you."

She gazed at him thoughtfully. There was no doubt that something had put him in a black mood. She thought back over the last hour and couldn't decide what might have done it. But whatever the cause, the mood seemed to have created a raw, pure form of sex appeal in him that intensified his masculinity and literally made her knees go weak. But she'd learned, and this time she didn't say what she was thinking. "You want me to lean over the sink?"

He nodded curtly. "This shouldn't take long."

"Whatever you say." She crossed the room to him, beginning to unbutton the shirt as she came.

"What are you doing?" he asked sharply.

She stopped, startled. "I'm sorry. I didn't ask first, but I chose another shirt out of your closet. I hope you don't mind, but they're so comfortable and—"

"I mean," he said with exaggerated patience, "why are you unbuttoning that shirt?"

"To keep it from getting wet while you shampoo me," she said reasonably. With over a third of the buttons undone, she lifted the neck of the shirt so that it fell off her shoulders and down her arms, and the bottom hem rose and parted, giving the slightest glimpse of her panties.

He practically broke his wrist twisting the faucet on. "This shouldn't take long at all," he muttered, aware that he was repeating himself.

She leaned over the sink, letting the counter support her weight. Since her hair was already wet, he squirted shampoo into the dark tresses and began working it in. But he had to stand close behind her in order to reach over her, and the feel of her exquisitely rounded backside pushing so temptingly against the lower portion of his body did nothing for his peace of mind.

"Brady, you're hurting me."

His fingers stilled on her head as he realized how hard he had been scrubbing her scalp. "Damn it, Marissa, *tell* me the next time I'm hurting you."

"I just did."

The unexpected dry humor he heard in her voice didn't improve his temperament, but he eased the pressure of his fingers to a gentle massage. Lather spread down her neck and onto her shoulders, luring his hands to follow the shampoo's path until he was lightly kneading her tense muscles with slow circular movements. And if at times the tips of his long fingers happened to graze the tops of her breasts, he told himself it was an understandable accident.

His calloused hands rasped over her skin, and Marissa shivered with pleasure. She felt the hard outline of his body against her back, and heat grew inside her that had nothing to do with the pressure of his fingers deep in the muscles of her shoulders. Blood beat in her ears. Excitement wound in her stomach. She wasn't ready for the delight to end when he poured a pitcher of warm water over her head, washing away the soap.

He wrapped a towel around her head and eased her upright. "How are you doing? Do you need to sit down?"

She *was* dizzy, but she wasn't sure of the cause. "I think I'd better."

He guided her into the living room and helped her to sit on the rug in front of the fire. "Since you can't raise your arms, I guess I'd better try to get those tangles out of your hair."

"I'm a lot of trouble," she said softly, the heat of the fire relaxing her.

Coming down behind her he pulled her in between his legs until her bottom once again nestled against the hard ridge of his manhood. And once again he had only himself to blame. It was as if he knew he couldn't go any further with her, he thought grimly, but he wanted to give himself the luxury of this one fairly innocent sexual contact—even though it increased his desire instead of easing it.

He guided the comb through the shining black length of her hair, taking care not to pull or tug. The gentleness of his action was in contrast to the gruffness of his voice. "Don't worry about it."

"But I've invaded your life, taken over your wardrobe—"

"I have more than a few flannel shirts, Marissa."

She had just showered. He knew she couldn't be wearing any perfume, and yet every time he leaned close to her, he caught a scent that was feminine, seductive, mind-bending.

"I know, I just meant . . . My gratitude makes you uncomfortable, doesn't it?"

"Your gratitude isn't necessary."

He'd tangled his hands in a woman's hair before while gripped by passion, but he could never remember shampooing or even combing anyone's hair. It was a type of intimacy he hadn't known existed, and it shook him more than his arousal.

Her hair felt and looked like wet silk, he decided.

"Nevertheless, when I get better, I'm going to do all I can to help you around the house."

"I have someone who comes up here once a week to clean the house." She tried to glance over her shoulder at him, but he stopped her with his hands. "Keep still or I'll never get through."

She didn't think twice about the curtness of his voice. "Then there has to be something else I can do."

"There is. Get well."

She gnawed thoughtfully on her bottom lip. "Will you sleep with me tonight?" She felt his body go stiff behind her. "What I mean is, will you hold me like you did last night?"

The movement of the comb stopped. "I don't think so."

"It would make me feel better."

"Last night I needed to wake you at regular

intervals. That's no longer necessary. You won't need me tonight."

But she did need him, she thought, in ways she couldn't explain because she didn't understand them herself. "Where will you be?"

"Down here on the couch. Don't worry," he said, getting to his feet. "It's comfortable, and I'll still be able to hear you if you call out."

Marissa rocked slowly back and forth in the big pine chair and smiled dreamily as her hand caressed the satin finish of the arm. Yesterday she had discovered Brady was more than someone to keep her safe from the storm, that in fact he was a man of immense sexual appeal. Today she had discovered the home of the man, and she decided she liked it very much.

There was nothing sleek or sterile about the two-story log and stone house. The rooms had warmth and color and a feeling of comfort that went beyond the deeply cushioned sofas and chairs: It was a comfort of the soul. Here a person could create or be at peace. Storms might rage outside, but inside there would always be safety and warmth.

Everywhere she looked she was entranced. A large hooked rag rug done in camel, oatmeal, and brown covered part of the wide planked floor. Several more like it were upstairs, she remembered, one even in the bathroom.

Two sofas and one chair were upholstered in blue tweed. A basket of pine cones and dried seed pods joined hand-wrought fireplace tools on the hearth. Her gaze came to rest on a soft-sculptured duck, its body brown calico and its head and wings solid blue, then moved to a wooden owl. Serenity and hominess surrounded her, soothing and beguiling her. She wanted to stay here forever, cocooned from all hurt and loneliness.

Hurt? Briefly she frowned. Had there been pain in that world outside, she wondered, then quickly smothered the thought and let the contentment once more flow back to enfold her.

When Brady came in the front door, she looked up and smiled brilliantly at him. "Has the rain stopped?"

He shrugged out of his denim jacket and hung it on a peg by the door. "Not really. A mist is falling right now." She was wearing another of his flannel shirts, he noticed, this one a deep purple, and he could tell by the way the flannel lay caressingly over the firm roundness of her breasts that the shirt and her panties were all she had on. She had chosen to be comfortable during her convalescence, and he supposed he couldn't blame her.

It wasn't her fault he couldn't take his eyes off her.

His gaze strayed to the creamy white skin of her throat left exposed by the open collar, then to the long, slender legs, and finally to her bare feet where the tufts of the shaggy rug curled sensuously around her toes. "The storm will be back though. We can count on it."

"Oh? How can you be sure?"

He ran his hands over his damp hair and

moved toward the fire. "Years of living on this mountain. Storms don't go away easily. They wander around gathering new strength, then they suddenly whip back on themselves."

She gave a sudden shiver and wrapped her arms around herself. "I don't like storms."

His eyes on her narrowed with interest, her reaction making him suddenly wonder if it was a storm other than the one in which she had got hurt that she might be remembering. "It's nothing to get upset over. Even if it comes back, you'll be safe."

"I know." Her arms tightened around her body. "I'm really very lucky."

"Lucky?" He gave a short laugh of disbelief. "You've just had a bad accident, you're lost, and you can't remember anything. I wouldn't call that lucky."

"I found you, didn't I?"

Heat coiled low in his body. In an effort to shake off the feeling, he took up a poker and jabbed at the big logs he had placed earlier at the back of the fireplace. "How long have you been up from your nap?"

She made a wry face. "My fourth nap of the day, you mean."

"Rest is the best medicine I can offer you. How long?"

"Only a little while. I was looking around your house, and do you know what I decided?"

"What's that?"

"I decided you must be a very tactile person."

He threw a glance over his shoulder, then

straightened and turned to her. "What makes you say that?"

She grinned. "Because you surround yourself with things that are eminently touchable."

He'd love to surround himself with her; the thought came against his will. "I do like to touch." He cleared the thickness from his throat and attempted to appraise her clinically. It was impossible. There was no doubt she was improving physically, and viewing her as a hurt child who needed his help was no longer possible. Still, he decided, her health would be a safe subject for them to discuss. "How are you feeling?"

"My headache's almost completely gone, but my mind is like the air outside—full of mist." She lowered her gaze to the fire, her contented mood abruptly gone.

Maybe another subject, he thought, dropping down on the cushioned couch. "Rodin's formed quite an attachment to you." The mention of the Irish setter brought a smile to her face, as he had intended.

"He's great company. I envy you having him. I've never had a dog."

He tensed. She had spoken casually, apparently unaware she had just recalled something. "You haven't?"

She shook her head. "No."

He made his tone deliberately low key. "I had a couple of dogs when I was growing up, but none since. Then one day a few years ago, I stopped by a friend's house in town. Several weeks before, his Irish setter had presented him with a whole litter of pups, and they were in a box out on his back porch." He waved his hand toward the dog, who had settled on the floor beside Marissa, his eyes contentedly closed. "Rodin was the runt, the puniest little thing you ever saw. He could barely walk, but as soon as he saw me he scrambled out of the box and followed me all around the house. By the time I left, it was clear I wasn't going to get out of there without him. I honestly think he would have followed me back up this mountain if I hadn't decided to take him home with me. My friend later told me that Rodin had been distinctly unresponsive when prospective buyers had come to look at him. Funny."

"Not really. He'd been waiting for you."

Her loving tone made him shift uncomfortably.

"You mentioned having pets when you were growing up," she said curiously. "Were you raised in this area?"

"Yes. Not too far from here."

"And your family?"

"My mother and father still live in the family home on the other side of town."

"Will I get to meet them?"

Amazed that for a moment he actually considered the idea, he shook his head. "I don't think so."

She tried to mask the sudden jab of pain his words brought. "I wonder if my parents are alive."

He gave a low curse as he saw her strained expression. "Marissa, I only meant that as soon

as the bridge is back in, I'm sure you'll be wanting to leave."

She lowered her lashes, veiling her eyes. "Yes,
of course." She lapsed into silence.

Brady watched her, frustrated at her distress.
If only he could help her more.

He found himself admiring the beautiful bone
structure of her face, the graceful arch of her
neck, the elegant lines of her body. Lord, he
thought, how he would love to sculpt those
lines, to search out and discover the secrets
behind that exquisite shell.

What would he find? What thoughts, what
dreams?

Whom would he find? What friends, what
family . . . what lovers?

He'd give a lot to know, he decided, but knew
he wouldn't find his answers by sculpting her.
As good as he was, he'd end up with only an
imitation at best. No living artist could create
something as beautiful as she was. So he waited.

In the end, Rodin snapped her out of her
reverie by putting his head on top of the seat
cushion and nuzzling her knee, begging wordlessly to be petted. She obliged. "You're a good
dog, aren't you?"

Rodin's tail swished wildly back and forth,
indicating his agreement.

She glanced over at Brady. "Where did you go
while I was napping?"

"I had to check on some things out in the
shop."

"I'm keeping you from your work."

She sounded so stricken, he had to laugh.

"Don't worry about it. If I wanted to work, I'd be doing it. Right now, though, I think it's more important that I keep an eye on you."

"You've been wonderful to me, and I'm not even sure I'll ever be able to pay you back."

He straightened. "You don't owe me a thing, Marissa, now or in the future. When you finally remember, and you will, I want you to remember *that*."

There was something about his intent stare that made heat come up under her skin. But she wasn't put off by her response to him, just as she wasn't intimidated by his brusqueness. She accepted him as if she'd known him all her life. And why not? No matter what had gone before, her life *had* begun the moment he had opened the door and brought her in from the storm.

"I'd like to see your workshop," she said.

He shrugged. "Maybe when you're stronger."

"All right." She watched him for a little while. "I seem to remember your telling me you built this house yourself."

He nodded. "I did tell you that. I was trying to reassure you about the storm."

"Did you really build it?"

"Yeah. Fifteen years ago I had houses in L.A. and New York. But . . . I decided I needed to come home. I bought this land and set to work. I watched the stones being quarried, and I split the logs myself. I even learned to do wiring and plumbing. Foot by foot I built it."

She smiled softly at the satisfaction she heard in his voice. "It's a beautiful house."

"I never worked so hard in my life, but I enjoyed every minute of it. And I needed it."

"Why is that?"

He hesitated. "Sometimes you can lose sight of what's really important. Coming back to this mountain, building this house brought me back to reality."

"Reality." She murmured the word as if she were hearing it for the first time. "I like your reality, and I like the way the house is decorated. Did you do it?"

He laughed. "It's not decorated."

Briefly she wondered why she'd used that word. "I guess what I meant was, did you choose all the furniture and things?"

"Yes, I chose what made me comfortable. And I made that chair you're sitting in, along with several other pieces. Some of the other things were made by local artisans, like the rugs, the soft sculptured duck, the wrought-iron fireplace tools."

She stroked the palm of her hand up and down the chair arm. "I've always loved rocking in front of a fire. Do you like it?"

"Yes," he said, suddenly careful. Twice in a short space of time she'd made reference to something as if it were a memory. He waited to see what would happen next.

"When I was a little girl, I used to have a red rocking chair. I'd—" She broke off, one hand flying to her temple. She looked at him with alarm. "What happened, Brady? There was something there. It was *there*. Now there's only blankness."

"Don't try to force it."

"But I was remembering. There was this picture of a red rocking chair in my mind, but it's not there anymore, and I don't know what I was about to say."

He bolted off the couch, knelt in front of the chair, and took her arms in his hands. "It's all right, Marissa. It's all right. It will come back, but you can't force it. Forget about it for now. Think about something else. About Rodin. This room. Anything."

She let out a shaky breath. His nearness dispelled the agitation of her mind, replacing it with a disturbance of the senses. She reached out and touched his face. "You. You fill my mind now."

He almost groaned. Well, he had said *anything*. "You have to stop saying things like that."

"Why?"

"Because you're not yourself."

"If I were well and I still said those things, what would you do?"

His jaw clenched, and his thumbs restlessly rubbed her shoulders. "The answer to that depends on too many things that I don't know."

Clouds gathered in the amethyst depths of her eyes as she stared back at him. "Do you think I was coming to see you when I had my accident?"

"At first I did. When you opened your eyes and looked at me you said, 'Thank God I found you.' "

"I did?"

"You said it twice. Do you have any idea what you might have meant?"

"No. I don't even remember saying it."

"It doesn't matter," he said, except he had a strange feeling it *did* matter. His gaze dropped to her mouth.

Her tongue flicked across the bottom lip, leaving behind a moist sheen. "Are there any people who live close by? Anyone I could have been going to see?"

He pulled his hands away but didn't move from in front of her. "No. After you cross the bridge, there's only my property, and I wasn't expecting company that night. But that doesn't mean anything. You could have lost your way in the storm and taken a wrong turn on your way to any number of places."

She had a deep need to believe she was somehow connected to him. "But maybe I *was* looking for you."

"And maybe you weren't, Marissa. Remember the credit card I found with your name on it?" She nodded. "Well, the chief of police is trying to trace it for me. Sometime tomorrow we may know where you live."

A troubled look came over her face.

In that moment, Brady believed he knew what she was feeling, because to his astonishment, he'd just discovered that he didn't want Tom to find out who she was or where she was from. He wanted to keep her all to himself.

What a selfish bastard he was.

What a completely normal man he was.

What a strong person he was going to have to be.

"What happens if he's able to trace the card?" she asked.

"Tom will contact the police station nearest your address to see if anyone has reported you missing."

"And if they have?"

He exhaled a long breath. "Then they'll be notified, and I imagine they'll come to get you as soon as possible."

Her anxiety was marked with a frown. "But they'll have to wait until the bridge is rebuilt, won't they?"

"Yes."

"Then I hope that takes forever."

"That's because you can't remember anyone yet. All you know is me."

"You're all I want to know." Suddenly, without her thinking, the words tumbled out. "I love you, Brady."

He went pale. "You don't know what you're saying."

"Yes, I do," she said, quietly sure. "I didn't realize it until just this moment, but it doesn't make it any less the truth. I love you."

"For heaven's sake, you only showed up on my doorstep two days ago. It's too soon for you to have any feelings for me. Hell, you don't even know me."

"But I do know you. I know you're kind and you're gentle and—"

"Kind?" he asked roughly. "I'm a lot of things, Marissa, but kind is not one of them. And Lord knows I'm not gentle. I'll be damned if I'll let you make me into a hero I'm not and then blame me later when I don't live up to the image."

"You could never disappoint me."

He stifled a groan. What sane man would push away a woman who looked at him as if she believed he could turn back the tides? Did a well even exist from which he could draw that much strength?

"Listen to me, Marissa. A baby duck will bond to the first thing it sees when it hatches out of its shell. That's exactly what you've done. You opened your eyes to a new world and you saw me. You were frightened, so you latched onto me, which, let me tell you, is damned ironic. I could give you the names of women who would tell you that I'm not safe at all. But it doesn't matter. Your amnesia is not going to last, and we need to find out who you are."

"Why?"

Her plaintive question affected him more than he would have thought possible. "Because sooner or later you're going to learn that I'm not the only man in the world. For my mental and physical health, it would be better if it were sooner." He slid his hand inside the collar of the shirt and cupped the side of her neck.

The contact produced a heat that took her breath away, and she wanted more than anything to believe that he felt the same wonderful way. "And what if there *is* a man in my life, Brady?"

"Then, honey, I'm going to stay the hell away from you."

She swallowed hard; her eyes were wide and entreating. "Could you?"

"I would do it or die trying."

"It sounds to me like it would be hard for you to leave me alone."

He groaned. "Drop it, Marissa."

"I want you, Brady."

His hand contracted on her neck. His jaw tightened. His words came out fiercely. "You wouldn't even know who you were if I hadn't told you. You sure the hell don't know what wanting is."

"It's what I'm feeling. It's heat and heaviness. It's softness and fire."

"Stop it."

"It's you—"

His mouth came down on hers with all the pent-up desire that was in him. For one extraordinary moment he let himself go. He held her face still and thrust his tongue deep into her mouth. Great shudders of emotion shook his body. She was clinging to him. She was the most willing, giving woman he had ever known.

She was in essence granting him carte blanche with her. She'd let him do anything. If he let himself think about it too long, the power could easily go to his head and warp his sense of right and wrong. It could drive him crazy. She *was* driving him crazy.

Even now, as he reached out and curved his hand around her breast, she made a sound of pleasure. But who in her other life had kissed her, touched her, made love to her until she was senseless, as he so desperately wanted to do?

Maybe even more important, what—who—would she be when she regained her memory?

Tremors racked his body, and as he pulled away from her, a new, incredibly powerful reason for wanting her to remember suddenly came to him.

It was vitally important that they be on equal footing.

Because until her memory returned, and she was fully aware of what she was doing and why she was doing it, the restraints he would have to impose on himself were going to be sheer unadulterated hell.

Four

"... finally the credit card company was persuaded to cooperate," Tom said. "They gave me the mailing address. Luckily it's a street number, not a post office box—oh, and it's in Dallas. I notified the police department in her area. They recognized her name immediately, said she gets quite a few mentions in the society pages, but they hadn't had any missing person reports on her. I asked them to send a car by the address and notify anyone there that she's safe. Over."

Unaware of how tightly his hand was gripping the radio microphone, Brady said, "Was there anyone there? Over."

"Don't know yet. Haven't heard back, but I'll let you know as soon as I do. How is she? Over."

"Better. I want her checked by a doctor as

soon as the bridge is repaired, but I think she's going to be fine. It's just the damn amnesia . . ." He trailed off, then caught himself. "Thanks, Tom. Keep me informed. Over."

He leaned back in the chair and rubbed at his eyes. For the moment at least, Marissa didn't care who or what she had left behind, but that was because she was frightened. *He* wanted her to remember.

His thoughts became arrested. She was frightened. She had opened her eyes, looked at him, and said, "Thank God I found you." Since at that moment her mind was a blank slate, the words had to have come from her subconscious.

He frowned. Dammit, he wasn't thinking straight. Her meaning was simple: She was thankful she had found him because if she hadn't she might have died out on the mountain.

But if the reason was that uncomplicated, why was she still clinging to him as if she were in danger of drowning? It was almost as if she believed he was the one person in the world who could save her. It didn't make sense. She was safe now.

Or was she?

He sprang up and began pacing the room. Was it possible that she was in some sort of danger? Danger came in many forms. What could be so awful she'd blocked out her memory of it? The police in her area were apparently aware of nothing out of the ordinary, or they would have told Tom. So what or whom was she avoiding?

He stopped in the middle of the room and

forced himself to draw three deep breaths. He had all the patience in the world for his work, though it was a slow process to cut, chisel, and smooth a piece of wood into the image in his mind. But his tolerance for waiting for Marissa to regain her memory had fallen below zero.

He wanted her completely well; he wanted to be sure that she was in no danger; and then he wanted her gone from his life. That's what he wanted.

He turned on his heel and went in search of her.

He found her in the kitchen, staring with fascination at his old waffle iron as it oozed and bubbled waffle batter all over the counter. "What are you doing?"

She turned to him, a lopsided smile on her face. "I've just discovered something about myself. I can't cook. Or at least, I can't make waffles."

He walked to the counter and unplugged the waffle iron. "What are you doing in here, anyway? If you were hungry, all you had to do was say something."

"I didn't want to bother you. Besides, I'm stronger now. I should be trying to stay up for longer periods of time." She trailed her finger through a puddle of batter and stuck it into her mouth. "I came in here and found the box of waffle mix and the waffle iron. The directions looked easy enough. The batter tastes fine. I don't know where I went wrong." She scooped another fingerful of batter off the counter and held it up to his mouth. "You try it."

"Uh, no, thank you." Her finger in his mouth wasn't the best idea in the world, he decided, then watched, mesmerized, as she shrugged, slid the same finger into her mouth, and sucked off the batter. Tearing his gaze away from her, he lifted the top of the waffle iron. "Looks to me like you poured in the whole recipe. You should have used half a cup at a time. A cup at the most."

"Oh." She gnawed thoughtfully on her bottom lip, then asked, "I wonder if it's really possible that I don't know how to cook?"

"I don't know." He reached around her for a dishrag and accidentally brushed the softness of the flannel shirt she was wearing and the breast beneath. He waited a beat for the flare of heat to die down. "Does it really matter?"

"I guess I'm curious."

He wiped the excess batter away from the rim of the waffle iron, then looked at her. "You said yesterday that you didn't want to remember."

Uncertainty formed in her eyes. "I don't. It's only that—heavens, you'd think I could cook. Everyone can, can't they?"

"Not everyone. And anyway, maybe you can cook. Maybe you're just rusty." He tossed down the rag.

"Why would I be out of practice? Do you think I ate out all the time?" She rubbed fretfully at her forehead.

He leaned his elbow on the counter so that their faces were even. "Marissa, I spoke with Tom a few minutes ago."

She tensed. "Tom?"

"Tom Harris, the local chief of police I told you about earlier. Through the credit card number, he's been able to get your mailing address." The sudden paling of her face stopped him. "What's wrong?"

"I don't want to hear this."

"Before you get any more upset, let me tell you I haven't really found out anything. All I know is the mailing address is in Dallas. They're going to send a car by the address."

"I *told* you I didn't want to know." Her eyes teared and her voice broke.

He pulled her into his arms. "Oh, God, Marissa, I wish you could tell me why you don't want to remember who you are."

"I just have no need to know what's over that bridge," she mumbled against his chest. "Can't you accept that and what I *can* tell you? I love you."

Her womanly curves pressed against him, making his body respond in ways he couldn't cope with. He unclasped her hands from behind his back and pushed her away. "This is not fair to either of us."

"Why? It's fair to me. It's what I want."

"You've lost every guard and protective device life has given you up to this point. I can't let myself take advantage of you. Try to understand."

Marissa studied his hard face. The impression of coldness in his eyes had turned to a heated storminess. "I understand that you're an honorable man."

"I'm a *man*, Marissa. That's the bottom line. That's all you should be concerned with. I'm no hero. I've done what any other person would have done under the circumstances. You were hurt and needed help. I took you in and did what I could. No big deal."

"No big deal as far as it goes, Brady, but I fell in love with you. I didn't plan to. It happened fast, but it didn't happen all at once. I opened my eyes and saw someone I could trust with my life. Hours passed. You took care of me. You held me through the night. You fed me. You shampooed my hair. You kissed me. And all of a sudden I realized that I was in love with you."

A soft rain had begun to beat against the kitchen window. He raked his hands through his hair, trying to ignore the tears that were forming in her eyes. "That's not a lot to base love on."

"Maybe not, but I'll bet some people go their whole lives and never experience the tenderness and love you showed me during those hours."

"Tenderness and love? Marissa, I told you—"

"I know—you're not gentle or kind. And maybe you aren't, by most people's standards. What matters is you are to me. I'm sorry if that upsets you or embarrasses you. And I'm sorry if I'm being a lot of trouble." The tears escaped and rolled down her face. "And if it'll make you happy, as soon as that damn bridge is repaired, I'll leave."

His resolve was not strong enough to withstand the amethyst eyes shimmering with tears. He drew her back into his arms. "Don't you know what you do to me?" he muttered roughly.

"Don't you know that I can't get near you without wanting to—"

She stood on her tiptoes and pressed her lips to his, and when his tongue thrust hungrily into her mouth, a deep satisfaction shuddered through her. She didn't know how she knew it, but somehow, in some distant time and place, she had been made for this man. Her body didn't need to adjust to his when he held her. As soon as she felt his heat, her bones seemed to mold themselves to conform to his. And when they kissed, her blood turned to fire.

She understood that he didn't love her. Now. But it stood to reason that if she had been made for him, he had been made for her. He couldn't remain unaffected by her love. Someday soon, with or without the bridge being repaired, he would love her.

His hand slipped beneath the hem of her shirt, then upward till it closed around the fullness of her breast. He felt her uncontrollable shiver at the contact, felt her go weak against him, and knew he should stop. Instead he gathered her more tightly to him. The hardened nipple nestled in the middle of his palm. "You make me insane," he muttered, dropping feverish kisses over her face and down her neck. "We can't do this. We shouldn't—"

"Do you want to make love to me?"

"Dear Lord, yes."

"Then how can it be wrong?"

"Marissa, no. It is . . ."

He tried to push her away, but suddenly he had grown weak and she had grown strong. Or maybe he hadn't really tried to push her away at all. He wasn't sure.

His brain was scrambled, his thought processes destroyed. Thunder rolled up the mountain. Rain pelted against the window. Marissa made a small sound. His loudly pounding heart mixed with the noise of the approaching storm, creating a din in his ears, and suddenly he wasn't sure whether she had made a cry of passion or of fear.

The idea that it could be fear sparked a determination he hadn't known he possessed. Slowly, shakily, he moved away from her. Getting his bearings, he passed his hand over his eyes.

Standing alone now, without support, Marissa wrapped her arms tightly around her body, a defense against the shock of pain and confusion that threatened to engulf her.

Brady dropped his hand from his eyes. And his heart turned over. There was a new guardedness about her, the first he had seen in her since she had awakened to her fresh clean world, a guardedness *he* was responsible for. To him it almost seemed a scar on something otherwise perfect. "Try to understand, Marissa."

She pushed her hair away from her face with an unsteady hand and gave a short laugh. "You say that a lot, and as a matter of fact, I don't want to hear it anymore."

He extended his hand, then let it fall to his side. "I'm sorry. I really am. This is for your own good."

An odd expression came and went in her eyes. "I think my mother used to say that to me. I don't think I liked it any more then than I do now. I'm going upstairs."

The storm rumbled around the mountain all evening long, receding for a while, then returning. With only Rodin for company, Marissa stayed in the bedroom, her tension ebbing and flowing with the thunder and the rain. When the storm was directly overhead, she paced. When it moved away, she sat by the bedroom fire and stared into the dancing flames, finding shapes and forms within the bright-colored blaze, but no answers.

There was a new uneasiness she couldn't trace, but even with all the unanswered questions, she did manage to come to a decision. She had to stop throwing herself at Brady. His rejection had crushed her, and her boldness made him unhappy, driving a wedge between them.

Around eight o'clock, Brady interrupted her solitude. "I've brought you a tray."

She glanced up, indifferent to the idea of a meal. "You shouldn't have bothered. I'm not really hungry."

He walked across the room and placed the tray on the end of the bed. "You need to eat." He shoved his hands into the pockets of his jeans and gazed unseeingly around the bedroom. He wanted to say something to her—needed to, really—but no words came to him. In truth there was nothing casual he could say, nothing that wouldn't be threatening or upsetting to her. "Are you all right? I mean, do you have everything you need?"

"I'm fine."

Her coolness cut him. Hidden in his pockets, his hands balled into fists. "I'll be out in my workshop if you need me. Just open the door and tell Rodin to get me." He waited, but when she didn't say anything, he left the room.

Marissa only picked at the food. An hour later she carried the still-full tray downstairs and placed it on the kitchen counter. Then drawn to the window over the sink, she gazed out. About seventy-five yards away, lights glowed from the windows of a large building. She stood there for a long time in the dark kitchen, looking toward the light. When after a while there was no sign of Brady, she made her way back upstairs and to bed.

The storm raged around her. The thunder was deafening, the lightning blinding. God, she was all alone. But there had been someone else . . . a man. Where was he? Why didn't he help her?

She clutched at her stomach. The pain, low inside her, was excruciating. Terrified, she called out for help. There was no one to hear, no one to care. Tears soaked her face. The rain beat against the metal roof. Lights flashed. Why had he left her all alone?

She was trapped. Trapped . . .

Hands pulled at her.

"Wake up, Marissa. Wake up. You're having a bad dream."

Brady's voice reached her through the storm. She opened her eyes and sobbed with relief when she saw his hard face above her. "Oh, thank God." She sat bolt upright and threw her arms around him. He was bare-chested, warm and strong. She clung to him.

He kissed the top of her head. "It's over now. You're safe. It was just a dream."

She moved her face against the warm column of his neck and heard the distant sound of thunder. "It was the storm."

"It was pretty bad there for a while, but it's moved on down the mountain. It probably won't be back."

She drew away, her tear-drenched eyes filled with apprehension. "No, you don't understand. There was a storm in my dream."

He smoothed his fingertips over her face, wiping away her tears. "That's natural. You were trapped out on that mountain in a hell of a storm, but—"

She grabbed his big wrist, stilling his fingers. "*No!* I wasn't trapped outside. I was trapped *inside*."

His brow pleated in puzzlement. "What are you talking about?"

"The storm in my dream was a different storm than . . . I don't know. I was *inside* something."

He slowly lowered his hand between them, but she kept hold of his wrist. The contact and the strong, steady beating of his pulse reassured her. Brady was rock solid, the one thing in this world she could depend on.

"Have you remembered anything, Marissa?"

She shook her head, agitated and vehement. "No. I'm just telling you, this was a *different* storm. And I don't know what it means!"

"Okay, okay," he said, his voice soft, soothing. "Relax. It's nothing to worry about. Dreams hardly ever make sense anyway. They're like mismatched jigsaw pieces. It's impossible to make a clear picture out of them. Don't turn yourself inside out trying to find a meaning when there isn't one."

"But—"

"Lie back down." He took her by the shoulders and lowered her head to the pillow.

Instead of calming her, his action made her break out in a cold sweat. "Brady, please don't leave me!"

Compassion filled his heart. He leaned over her, placing a hand on either side of her head. "Marissa, I can't stay here with you, but I'll be downstairs. I can hear you if you call."

"I won't stay here without you." Her throat ached as she held back new unshed tears, but her expression was set with determination. "If you go downstairs, I'll follow you. Please, Brady. I don't want to dream again, and I won't if you hold me."

He groaned. "My holding you has nothing to do with your dreaming."

"Maybe you're right. But what if you're not? I don't think you are, and I don't want to take a chance. At any rate, am I asking so much?"

Yes, he thought. *You're asking for comfort, when what I want to do is make love to you.* He sighed. He had no choice. "All right."

He slid off the bed, switched off the light, then returned to her. Stretching out on top of the covers, he took her into his arms.

Marissa settled stiffly against him, her face resting against his bare chest. At first she found it impossible to relax. Her dream played through her mind like the frames of a movie. She shifted nervously in his arms. Without saying anything, he began stroking his fingers through her hair. After a while, the combing motion began to relax her. She focused on the sound of his heartbeat beneath her ear, and slowly the tension drained out of her muscles.

But an unexplained uneasiness lingered. Out of the mist of her mind, shadows had begun to take form.

Right before she dropped off to sleep, she murmured, "There was a man in my dream, Brady . . . and he wasn't you."

His fingers stilled in her hair.

After the disturbing night, Marissa slept late the next morning, and when she awoke, Brady was gone. She stretched and turned her head toward the window. The day was overcast, but all signs of rain had disappeared.

She rose and showered, then without being entirely certain why, she dressed in her own clothes. They were a link to the past she wanted to remain buried, yet she felt compelled to put them on this morning.

She had no answers, only questions, but her mind was no longer like a pool of mirror-calm water. Ripples of disquiet disturbed the surface, making her anxious about what lay beneath.

More than ever she wanted the wooden bridge to remain impassable so that she could stay with Brady, but she was being drawn toward remembering, and there didn't seem to be anything she could do about it.

After several days of wearing little more than Brady's flannel shirts, the cream-colored silk blouse and linen trousers seemed uncomfortable. But at least, she thought, gazing into the mirror, her image seemed more familiar. She even felt a certain sense of satisfaction that the scratches on her face had almost disappeared and the swelling on her forehead had gone down, leaving behind a purplish bruise that would also be gone soon.

Brady received something of a shock when Marissa came downstairs. The last few days he'd spent a lot of his time trying to deal with the earthy kind of sexiness she exuded as she'd padded around his house barefoot, wearing little more than one of his shirts. Now, dressed in her stylish and obviously expensive clothes, with her hair brushed and waving softly around her face and shoulders, there was an added dimension of allure about her that he found gut-wrenching. But he took great care that nothing of what he was feeling showed. "I've just spoken with Tom Harris again."

Her head came up like a deer sensing danger.

"Last night's storm was more wind than rain, and the river has gone down. Enough so that they'll start working on the bridge."

"How long will it take them?"

"It should be passable by tomorrow." He paused. "They spotted your car about a mile downstream. There's no doubt about it. If you hadn't gotten out, you would have drowned, Marissa."

She waited for the terror she must have felt to come back to her. There was nothing.

When she didn't say anything, he continued. "Also the police have checked out the address. The house was empty, but the police spoke to a couple who live in a cottage on the grounds."

"Couple?" she asked, searching her mind, but coming up with no clue whom he could be talking about. "Who are these people?"

"They work for you and have for several years. According to them, you left Dallas Friday, heading for a cabin you had arranged to rent in this area. They said you often went off alone for weeks at a time and that's why they hadn't been worried."

Swallowing hard, she sank into a chair. "What else did they say?"

He knew exactly what she was asking. "You're not married, but they didn't know for sure whether or not there was anyone of significance in your life."

"You mean a man."

"That's right," he said, watching her carefully. "It seems there are quite a few men who escort you to various functions around Dallas."

"Sounds like a fun time," she said in a voice that indicated otherwise.

Implacably he went on. "The good news is

that you apparently have lots of money. In fact, I can't find a piece of bad news anywhere in this information."

She rubbed her forehead. "No, I suppose not. And now at least I'll have some place to go when the bridge is repaired, won't I?"

A muscle in his jaw clenched and unclenched. "About that bridge . . ."

Her gaze locked on him. "What about it?"

"I want us to go down there today. I'm hoping that you'll see something that will trigger your memory and bring everything back."

"You really can't wait for me to be gone, can you?"

"Don't look at the situation that way. When your memory comes back, you're going to see everything a lot differently. Right now—"

"—I'm not being fair to you," she said, finishing his sentence for him.

"I was thinking more that you weren't being fair to yourself."

She felt nothing but resignation. "I'll go with you to the bridge."

Five

"Are you warm enough, Marissa?" Brady asked, taking the big four-wheel-drive Jeep slowly around a curve. He had no desire that the trip down the mountain should frighten her. "We can put up the window."

"No, the wind feels good. Besides," she said, "I do have on three layers."

He glanced at her and saw the tension etched in her face, and his hands tightened on the wheel with frustration. If only there were some way he could make this whole thing easier for her. He couldn't though, just as he couldn't seem to make things any easier for himself. If only he could allow himself to accept the love she so badly wanted to give him, for the time it would last. . . . But it wouldn't be right. And in the end he would feel too much guilt if he let anything happen between them.

She was too open; he was too closed. She would eventually remember and leave. And he wouldn't be able to forget.

He looked over at her once more. He had insisted that she put a flannel shirt over her blouse and wear one of his denim jackets over that. Most women would have been lost in the oversized, masculine ensemble, but somehow the outfit came off as high style on her. He grinned. "One thing we know for sure about you, Marissa Berryman. You wear clothes well, no matter what they are or how many there are."

She was caught off guard, and warmed. His grin reminded her that no matter what would happen in the next few minutes at the river, he would be with her. As he had been from the first.

Some people might say she knew little more about him than she did about herself. But she knew all she needed to. He was a moody man who lived on top of a mountain alone, yet he had turned his life inside out taking care of her. And he made her feel incredibly safe and secure.

Last night he had gone to his workshop rather than stay in the same house with her, but first he had brought her food. Today he wanted her out of his life, but he was worried that she might be cold. And even now she sensed he was driving more slowly than he would if she weren't with him.

The last couple of days she had learned to live with the sadness of knowing that he didn't feel the same way about her that she did about him. Still, her opinion of Brady McCulloch hadn't changed. She loved him, she trusted him, she wanted him.

She felt at peace on this mountain with him, felt a bone-deep serenity in his home. She'd be content to stay there forever with him with no other memories than the ones they made together. But it seemed she wasn't going to get her way in this, and she struggled to accept this fact.

Above them, the sky was clearing, revealing patches of blue. Around them, fiery reds, yellows, golds, and bronzes flared against the evergreen of the pines. This mountain had nearly cost her her life, but with Brady beside her, she could appreciate its beauty.

She threw a glance over her shoulder at Rodin and laughed. His head was stuck out the window, his face pointed into the wind. "He's in dog heaven, isn't he?"

Brady nodded in agreement. "He loves riding in the Jeep. And he'll enjoy the next few hours. He hasn't really had a good run for several days now."

"You're going to let him run loose?"

The lines in his face crinkled with humor. "Rodin knows this mountain as well as I do. He'll come home this evening after he's had his fill of exploring." Brady down-shifted the Jeep, and his voice changed to one of warning. "The river and bridge are just around this next bend."

She straightened, mentally bracing herself, but when the rolling brown water and the wooden bridge came into view, she felt nothing more than idle curiosity at seeing something new.

He pulled the Jeep off to the side of the road and switched off the engine. As soon as the vehicle stopped, Rodin bounded out the window. Marissa's gaze followed the Irish setter until he disappeared into the trees. She envied the uncomplicated enjoyment that would be his over the next few hours.

Brady touched her arm. "How're you doing?"

She looked back at him with a smile. "So far so good."

"Up to getting out and walking around?"

"Sure. That's what we're here for, isn't it?"

Somehow her determined cheerfulness made him feel worse about this little field trip. What if he was wrong in trying to make her remember? He grabbed her hand as she opened the door. "We don't have to do this, Marissa."

She looked at him oddly. "I thought you said—"

"Never mind what I said. If this is too traumatic for you, we'll forget it right now."

Her expression softened at his concern. "Thank you, Brady. I appreciate that, but I'm fine, really."

Dammit, he thought, now she was comforting him. He must be really losing it. "Okay, then, let's go."

They climbed out of the Jeep, Marissa scrambling down on the opposite side and walking around to Brady. He gave a wave to the men who were working on the bridge, then, surprising her, he took her hand.

"Let's go downriver," he said.

"Is that the direction they found my car in?"

He nodded, his face grim as he thought of what she'd had to go through that night. "I'm sure the storm limited your visibility. You were unfamiliar with the roads here. You drove onto the bridge not knowing the danger and went right through the railing and into the river. You were damn lucky to have gotten out."

A cold shiver skipped down her spine. "I guess I was."

"You must also be a powerful swimmer. When this river gets going, the current is strong."

"Maybe I was just desperate."

His hand tightened on hers, anger rising in him. "Why in hell didn't you stop somewhere when the storm started, Marissa? Why did you try something that foolish and dangerous?"

She deflected his ire with calm. "I'd obviously never been in a storm on this mountain before. Then I got lost. I probably figured that turning around on this narrow road would be more dangerous than going straight ahead."

"Nothing could have been more dangerous than what you did," he said with real feeling.

"But I didn't know that, did I?"

"No, I guess you didn't."

They fell into silence as they walked along the bank of the river, following its path around a curve and out of sight of the bridge. The water rolled past them in a boiling rush. In contrast, they made their way slowly, the muddy patches of ground and their contemplative mood reflecting their caution.

Even so, it took only a momentary lapse of concentration and her foot slipped on a loose rock.

He caught her to him, preventing her fall. "Be careful," he murmured huskily, his glittering gray eyes moving over her hair, her eyes, and finally her face. In daylight, without make-up, her skin absolutely glowed. He released her.

They continued on, and his thoughts turned to the flannel shirts she'd been wearing. Would he leave them in the closet after she'd gone? Or would he banish the memories of her in them by wearing them? What would it be like, he wondered suddenly, to put on one of the shirts and have her scent and her feel against his skin?

Her steps gradually slowed, then stopped. "It's not the river or the bridge."

He mentally shook himself. "What?"

"I feel nothing when I look at either the river or the bridge. They're not the trigger for my memory."

"Then it has to be the storm. You heard the storm in your sleep and dreamed of another storm."

She gazed up at him. "I was already upset when I went to bed, Brady. Maybe it didn't have anything to do with the storm."

He'd been upset, too, he thought. He'd worked for hours that night, but the pleasure he usually received from the feel of the wood in his hands hadn't come. Instead he had been able to remember only the pleasure he'd felt having her in his arms.

He took her by the shoulders and unconsciously drew her closer. "I know I hurt you yesterday afternoon, and I'm sorry. And just in case there's any doubt in your mind, I definitely wanted you. You'll never know how badly. But your dream confirmed that I was right to stop it before it went any further."

"My dream?" she said, confused.

"There was another man in the dream."

She felt like screaming at this obsession he had with her past. "He was there only briefly."

"But he's obviously significant to you or you wouldn't have remembered him when you woke up."

She studied him intently. "What are you afraid of, Brady? Is it me?"

His hands tightened on her arms, but he quickly released her with a little push. "I know what you are now, Marissa. You're soft and sweet and the most feminine creature I've ever known. So much in fact, you drive me wild."

Her face lit up with hope. "Then—"

He held up a hand, cutting her off in midsentence. "What I don't know is what and who you will be when you regain your memory."

"Then you *are* afraid of me."

"I'm not afraid of you. Just . . . wary."

"Wary and very selfprotective."

"I've learned to be."

"But there's no need."

"You're wrong, Marissa. Most people are selfprotective to one degree or another. I have to protect you because you're not able to protect yourself right now. But I also have to protect myself."

"You?"

"As much as you don't want to think about it, the fact is, you're only temporarily in my life."

"And that bothers you so much you feel the need to protect yourself." He cared about her. He *did*. Her breath rushed out with a cry, and she forgot all about her resolve not to throw herself at him. "But don't you see, it doesn't have to be that way. I've told you, I want to stay with you."

"Dammit, that's *now*. What about later? You own a big home in Dallas. The police there recognized your name from the papers, where you were written up in the society pages. That means you obviously lead an active life with friends, family, . . . maybe even lovers."

"Lovers? Plural?" She shook her head, and her long black hair moved in shimmering waves over her shoulders. "You can't think that about me."

He briefly squeezed his eyes shut and shook his head. "That came out wrong. But I'm sure there are people back there who mean a lot to you, and once you remember you'll want to return."

'I'm not stupid. I understand what you're saying. But dammit, Brady, have you once considered the possibility that you could be wrong about this?"

He rubbed the tension gathering at the back

of his neck. "No, I haven't, but, lady, let me tell you, I've sure as hell wanted to."

With clenched fists she launched herself at him. "Then do it, Brady. Please *do* it."

He struggled for a moment to keep them from falling over. "Marissa—"

"No! No more words. I'm tired of talking. And I'm tired of wanting you." She wound her arms around his neck and pulled his mouth down to hers.

Instantaneously, fire flared within Brady. A harsh sound of need escaped his throat. Lord, how much could he stand? He'd wanted her from the moment he'd first seen her amethyst eyes gazing up at him. He'd never had a woman light up for him like she did, melt at his touch like she did, go up in flames at his kisses like she did. But, heaven help him, he couldn't let this happen. . . .

She moved sensuously against him, fitting her shape to his, and slid her fingers beneath his sweater to the hard muscles of his back. "Just say yes," she whispered. "Just say—"

He wrenched away from her violently, stumbling backward. "Stop it, Marissa!"

Her hand flew to her mouth as she choked back a sob. She looked at him with huge, stricken eyes. Then she turned on her heel and took off running, heading toward the Jeep.

It had taken every ounce of grit and fortitude he possessed to tear himself away from her, and for a minute, agony kept him paralyzed. His body was racked by a need so great he felt incapable of even calling her name.

Then he saw her fall, and he was jolted into action. He started after her, but before he could reach her, she was up and running again. She reached the Jeep before he did and climbed into it.

He reduced his pace to a walk, attempting to get himself under control before he joined her. But, he decided, it was going to take more than a few moments of gulping in deep breaths of air to slow his heart rate and cool his blood.

He swung up into the seat and looked at her. "Are you all right?"

She laughed shortly. "You've really got to quit asking me that."

His hand shot out to cup her chin and turn her face to him. Mud streaked her cheek, neck, and hands. "Did you hurt yourself when you fell?"

"No." She jerked away from him. "Just leave me alone. Take me back to the house."

Leaving her alone was exactly what he wanted to do, but even though he switched on the engine, he perversely delayed setting the Jeep in motion. "In a minute."

Her eyes widened with angry disbelief. "*Now.* Lord, what more do you want from me? I just threw myself at you. I was so willing, I didn't even care where we were. I would have been ecstatic making love in the mud." She gave a shaky laugh. "You know what? Now that I think about it, you're probably absolutely right about my other life. I act like such a wanton with you, I must have scores of lovers back in Dallas waiting for me."

His teeth came together hard. "Don't say that."

"Why not? It's got to be true. I bet I've got one hell of a diary."

"Marissa . . ." He almost reached for her. He almost pulled her to him.

Her fingers scrubbed at her forehead. "Haven't I humiliated myself enough for one day? Take me back now or I swear I'll get out and walk."

The tires kicked up gravel and dirt as he shoved the Jeep in gear, wheeled it around, and jammed his foot against the accelerator, all thoughts of driving carefully lost amid the tumultuous emotions whirling around inside him.

At the house, she sprang out of the Jeep and was through the front door before he could stop her. With a muttered curse he followed her. He found her in the living room, struggling with the buttons on the flannel shirt. The denim jacket she'd been wearing was already in a heap on the floor where she'd flung it.

Her hair flowed forward, hiding her face as she bent her head to see what she was doing. "I don't know what's wrong with me. I can't seem to get out of this damn shirt. The buttons on the jacket were bigger, but these . . . "

Her obvious anguish sliced through him, adding to his pain. "Let me help you," he said, crossing to her.

"No, I can do it. I really can."

"Let me," he said huskily, brushing her hand away and starting with the top button.

His nearness was unraveling what little reserve Marissa had managed to gather. Her chest rose and fell raggedly as she struggled for breath.

He doesn't want me. He doesn't want me. She said the words over and over again in her head, trying to grasp any thread of sanity she could and to hold on. Somehow she had to fight her way out of the delirium of passion that was seizing her. *He doesn't want me.*

Dizzy, she swayed, the motion inadvertently pressing her chest against his hands.

Incredibly awkward and slow, he'd only been able to undo two buttons. She had better stand still because, Lord help him, the enticing feel of her fullness was threatening to take control of his body away from him.

His voice was hoarse with leashed desire. "I'm nearly through. Just another minute." Compulsively, as if they were acting on their own, his fingers stroked across her nipple.

She drew air in between her teeth with a soft, hissing sound as heat jolted through her. Had that been an accident? Or was he in some way trying to punish her for loving him? "Just hurry," she said, choking back a sob, feeling his fingers now at the button between her breasts.

"I'm trying, . . . but there's a thread or something caught around this button." It would be all right, he thought. Two layers of cloth lay between him and her. There was the flannel of his shirt and the silk of her blouse . . . and then there was her flesh. But still, he remembered, he had been able to feel the erotic stiffness of her nipple through the material. It was a feeling he wanted just once more. He rolled the edge of his hand across the shirt until he could feel the aroused peak again.

With a cry that signaled her near breakdown, she pushed his hands away and gazed up at him, hotly accusing. "What are you trying to do to me, Brady? You know how much I love you and want you. You've got to—Lord knows I've told you often enough. Do you want me to beg you? Is that it?"

Caught up in a daze of heat, he shook his head. "No, I—"

"I will, you know. I've done almost everything else, haven't I? What's one more disgrace?" She hooked her fingers beneath the edges of the shirt and yanked as hard as she could. Buttons flew everywhere. She repeated the action with the cream silk shirt.

And then he no longer had to imagine. The loveliness of her breasts was totally exposed to him—their skin milk white, their tips rosy pink.

"Okay, Brady," she whispered. "Here I am. Touch me, love me. For Lord's sake, please."

A fever had gripped him. He passed his hands across his eyes. "Marissa—"

"Do you want me to get on my knees? Is that it?"

A shock wave slammed through him. "No . . . no . . ." Beads of perspiration dampened his brow. His need for her was so great, words stuck in his throat.

"You bastard!" She spun on her heels and bolted for the stairs.

"Marissa . . ."

She heard her hoarsely whispered name, but

didn't care. Tortured beyond endurance, she was unable to take any more rejection. Upstairs, she blocked Brady out of her mind and concentrated on stripping off her remaining clothes. In the bathroom she turned on the shower full force. The need to cool her heated body was of paramount importance.

Brady slowly climbed the stairs, his lower body engorged and throbbing. He felt pain with every step he took, but the thought of Marissa's soft flesh drew him onward. Something had snapped inside him. His power to reason was gone. Nothing but extinguishing the fire that raged within concerned him now. On the landing he shrugged out of the sweater and pulled off his boots. He followed the trail of her clothing to the bathroom.

As if it were a penance, she stood beneath the rain of the water, feeling as though her skin were being flayed. Every nerve she possessed burned, sensitized almost beyond bearing. She was lost. Lost . . .

The shower door opened and Brady walked in, wearing only jeans. Without breaking stride he took her by the shoulders and pushed her through the water to the back wall. Crushing his mouth to hers, he caught her cry of surprise.

This was what he'd been wanting, he thought crazily. Needing. Her. Marissa.

He pressed his body down on her, pinning her to the tile wall, and cupped her breast with urgent pressure. Her skin was wet and slick and, oh, so desirable. The water beat against his broad back and soaked his jeans, but he felt only her.

He kissed her time after time, ravaging her mouth, then dragged his lips down the smooth column of her throat to the peak of her breast where the tantalizing nipple waited for him. He fastened on it and sucked with the desperation of a man parched by desire.

Marissa clung to him in ecstasy. She couldn't believe he had come to her, was actually here in the shower with her. She caught his head in her hands and brought his mouth back up to hers, and at the same time rubbed the lower portion of her body against the roughness of his jeans. She needed the contact, needed urgently to ease the aching.

He was beyond care or consideration. He knew what he had to have and he went after it. He pushed his fingers between her legs and into her, and she opened like a flower to him.

She writhed beneath his touch. "Oh, yes . . . Brady."

Her uninhibited response blasted fire through his body. He unzipped his jeans, shoved them down, then raised and wrapped one of her legs around his hips, and entered her. He thrust and thrust, rocking her up and down against the wall, until he was high inside her, and even then he kept thrusting. Rapture that seemed to have no limits scored through him again and again.

He could feel the tempest mounting in her, but he was nowhere near completion. The wait for her had built up a powerful need in him;

his passion was endless. When her shuddering release came, squeezing convulsively around him, it excited him further.

He stepped out of his clothes, lifted her out of the shower, and laid her down on the hooked shag rug of the bathroom floor. There he buried himself in her once again.

The shower misted out the open door; billowing steam engulfed them. The powerful movement of his hips brought her to a crest once more. Then again. And then finally him.

Shortly after midnight, Marissa lay beside a sleeping Brady, his arm holding her loosely. Something was disturbing her, something doggedly niggling at the edges of her consciousness. Unable to sleep, she let her mind float free, too tired and too sated to rein it in.

What was bothering her? she wondered drowsily. The passion she and Brady had shared during the preceding hours was everything she had expected. Actually it had been more. Much more. The only thing that could have made it more perfect would have been his telling her he loved her. But at least now he wouldn't want her to leave. She'd stay, and in time she was convinced he would come to love her as much as she loved him.

Her eyelids grew heavy, her dark dense lashes drifted down to cast shadows on her cheeks, and she floated somewhere between sleep and awareness, consciousness and unconsciousness. She heard the wind come up, and there was a splattering of rain against the window. Just enough to make the roads slick, she thought. They had to be more careful. Thunder rumbled and soon lightning lit up the room. . . . No— lightning lit up the *car*. She frowned.

The rain pounded against the metal roof of the car. There were loud sounds—a crash, a shattering of glass, a scream. Pain shot through her stomach. She couldn't move. She was trapped.

Then she saw him. He was walking away from her.

The flashing lights came later. And the strange faces.

She sat straight up in bed, her eyes wide open.

A sheen of sweat dewed her skin; tremors shook her limbs. She glanced toward the window. No lightning, no thunder, no rain. But it had been so clear in her mind, like a moving picture, and the picture wouldn't go away.

Then she understood. *It hadn't been a dream.*

The door in her mind opened, and everything came rushing back.

She slid off the bed, careful not to disturb Brady, and stole downstairs. For hours she sat in front of the fire. With Rodin at her feet, she went over and over the events of the last few days, comparing them with her life—her real life. One hard, cold fact kept reemerging.

She couldn't love Brady.

Brady awoke at dawn and, puzzled at her absence, went downstairs to find her.

"Marissa, what are you doing down here?"

"I couldn't sleep, and I didn't want to bother you."

"You should know by now that you wouldn't have bothered me." Alert and intense, he swept his gaze over her, taking in everything about her. Her face was paler than usual, her body taut, in the grip of some powerful emotion. "You let the fire die down," he said quietly. "You must be cold."

"No."

He tossed a couple of logs onto the smoldering embers and poked and prodded until the fire blazed to life again. Then he sat down beside her. "Something's happened, hasn't it?"

She nodded, not looking at him. "I've remembered . . . everything."

He'd done all he could think of to help her regain her memory, but he wasn't prepared. Blood came up and drummed in his ears. This was what he'd been wanting, but now that her memory was back, all he could think of, all he could wish for was for things to be the way they had been between them.

She reached down and patted Rodin's head in a remote, detached way. When she stopped, he made a whimpering sound, but she didn't appear to hear.

"I plan to make arrangements this morning for transportation home. I imagine Samsonville has a car rental place?"

"You're renting a car to go home?"

She nodded. "I may have to put it on your credit card, but I'll reimburse you as soon as possible—"

"To hell with all that. What about last night?" She didn't answer him, and her continued silence grew so loud Brady thought it would deafen him. "Look at me, Marissa." He turned her to face him and for a moment was transfixed by a coolness deep within the amethyst eyes that he'd never thought to see.

"Last night was wonderful, Brady, but it's over. I can get back to my own life now, and you can get back to work."

He felt as if he'd been hit in the solar plexus, and it was his turn to fall silent.

"It must be very satisfying to know that you were right all along."

He swallowed with difficulty and finally managed to speak. "Right?"

"You said that once I remembered; I'd want to go back. What can I say? You were right."

Fighting the unreality of hearing his words thrown back at him, he said, "Marissa, you told me you loved me." Damn! He sounded like he was pleading. Drawing on all his resources, he summoned pride and anger to his aid.

Abruptly she got up, stepped over Rodin, and walked a few feet away. "I'm sorry about that. It must have been very embarrassing for you."

"It was awkward at times," he said, slowly recovering, "but I managed."

Quiet and serious, she folded her hands in front of her and gazed down at them. "I can't thank you enough. You saved my life. There's nothing I can do to repay you, but—"

He waved her thanks aside. "There is just

one thing I'd like to ask you before you go, purely out of curiosity."

She stiffened, waiting, willing herself to be brave a little while longer.

"Is there a man at home, waiting for you?"

She raised her head and looked squarely at him. "No."

"Then why are you going?"

"Because I have to. Because it's best. Both for you and for me. Now if you'll excuse me, I'll go up and get my things together." Her head held high, she turned toward the stairs.

Six

Nothing had changed, Marissa thought, leaning back in the deep cushions of the couch in her living room in Dallas, idly sipping a cup of coffee. In many ways it was as if she had never been gone.

A stack of messages waited with invitations to parties and requests for her to help arrange a benefit or chair a committee. She felt weary just thinking about it, which was strange, because for years now she'd taken on any and all social obligations without so much as a blink. But she'd faced death and survived, she reminded herself, and it was bound to make her see things differently. Perhaps her efforts had become too scattered. Perhaps she ought to pick one charity and make it her own. She'd think about it.

And in the meantime . . . She gazed around

her, waiting for the quiet elegant beauty of her home to soothe her as it had always done.

Everywhere she saw her own hand at work. Cost had not been counted in attaining the effect she wanted. She had used the carpet, the walls, and most of the furniture to achieve a background of white. Then, depending on the season and her mood, she used cool colors sparingly to create picture-book settings that had been written up in many national publications.

Today, though, the satisfaction she usually experienced from her surroundings did not come. She turned her attention toward the silk-draped twenty-foot windows and beyond to the perfectly manicured lawns and gardens. But instead she saw a mountain ablaze with the colors of autumn. And atop the mountain, a house of logs and stone. And within that house, a man and a dog.

"Marissa, darling, I couldn't believe it when I heard you were back so soon." CeCe breezed into the room, all blond sophistication and enthusiastic energy.

CeCe Kavanaugh was not only a long-time friend, but she was also one of the nicest and most uncomplicated people Marissa knew. CeCe was just what she needed, Marissa decided. "The drums are working overtime. How did you find out?"

"Are you kidding? Your accident was written up in the paper. A reporter on the police beat picked up the story."

She groaned. "Great, just great."

CeCe plopped down on the opposite end of

the couch. "'Well, I wouldn't worry. The story was sadly lacking in details. It simply said you had gone to Arkansas for a vacation, got caught in a storm, and driven your car off a bridge, but that you managed to save yourself and were all right." She leaned forward. "To *think* what you've been through. How are you?"

Marissa made a sweeping motion with her hand that encompassed herself from head to toe. "As you can see, I'm fine. Would you like some coffee?"

"No, thank you. Lord, look at that bruise on your forehead. Yuk. Does it hurt very much?"

"Not anymore."

"Heavens, look at your nails." Her voice rose in horror. "You need to make an appointment right away."

"I'll take care of it. Listen, if you don't mind I'd rather talk about something else. I'm home now and I'd really like to forget the whole thing."

"Was it that bad?"

Marissa hesitated. "Yes and no." Once she found Brady, it had been wonderful. She pushed the thought from her mind and fixed a bright, determined expression on her face. "So, tell me everything that's been happening."

"Nothing much," CeCe said, clearly disappointed that Marissa wasn't going to be more forthcoming. "You've only been gone a little over a week."

"Come on," Marissa said encouragingly. "There must have been something."

"Well, . . . the Robertses had their annual party this year to benefit the homeless. But you know that since you were invited. You were missed, of course. No one, including me, understands why you go off alone like you do."

"Were Paul and Kathy there?"

"Yes, and I'll tell you what. Kathy Garth looks like a bloody walking advertisement for being pregnant. She's disgustingly radiant."

"And everyone's jealous, right?"

"Right. By the way, Tracy Wells was elected chairwoman of next year's heart benefit."

"Wonderful. She'll do a good job."

"I guess. But she'll have to go a long way to top the job you did two years ago." She made an abrupt gesture with an acrylic-nailed hand. "Okay, that's all the news I can think of, and I'm dying of curiosity. What happened to you?"

Marissa sighed. "It was just as the newspaper said. I ran the car off the bridge in the storm."

"It's a wonder you didn't drown. How did you save yourself?"

"I managed to get out of the car and swim for the bank. Then I found . . . a house with someone home. They took me in. . . ."

CeCe clucked her tongue. "You were so lucky. Who's 'they'?"

She should have known CeCe wouldn't let her get away with glossing over the facts. "A man," she said grudgingly. She'd barely allowed herself to think about Brady, much less talk about him. "Actually a very nice man."

CeCe rolled her eyes with exasperation. "For goodness sake, Marissa, I've had easier times at the dentist. Who was this very nice man?"

"Brady McCulloch."

"Brady McCulloch," CeCe said, repeating the name thoughtfully, then she straightened as if a bolt of electricity had shot through her. "Not *the* Brady McCulloch, the famous sculptor!"

Marissa looked at her, stunned. Of course he was *the* Brady McCulloch.

She remembered him telling her that he worked with wood, and that he had made the rocking chair along with some of the other pieces of furniture. And she remembered the workshop behind the house that she'd never got around to seeing. Somewhere in her mind she had known who he was, but it hadn't seemed significant.

Brady the man had been infinitely more important to her than Brady McCulloch the world-renowned sculptor.

"He lives in the Ozarks, you know," CeCe was saying, "and has for years, ever since he just up and disappeared from the social scene quite a few years ago." When Marissa didn't say anything, CeCe reached over and swatted her arm. "Well, is it the same Brady McCulloch?"

"Apparently it is."

Brady threw a chisel across the big workroom, narrowly missing a piece of beechwood on the far workbench. The chisel fell to the floor. He let out a string of curses, then rounded on Rodin, who was curled a safe distance away.

"Don't look at me like that."

Rodin put his head between his paws and gazed reproachfully at his master.

"She's been gone a week. It's over."

He stalked over to the chisel and bent to pick it up. His glance grazed the piece of beechwood, then came back to it. Each piece of wood had its own identity; in some it took longer to discern than others. He'd had the wood for several years, waiting for it to tell him what it should be. Many other woods also sat about, abiding in harmonic patience until the time he was able to glean insight into the form they would become.

This particular piece of wood had always interested him because it was not straight. From its base it rose in a gradual inward curve. He circled the table, his face a study in concentration as he looked at the wood from every angle. The idea of a woman turned inward on herself came suddenly to his mind.

Irritated, he swung away. "She changed," he muttered, voicing something that had been eating at him. "I knew she'd change when she got her memory back. I just didn't expect to be so damn right."

He returned to the large elmwood figure on which he had been working. This sculpture was in an early stage, and what it would become was a shape only in his head at this point . . . as was the mood the piece would eventually convey. Stormy.

He reached for a rasp. What was he doing? He didn't want a rasp. He flung the tool aside. If he wasn't careful, he would ruin this piece.

"She had such a giving way about her," he mumbled. "Such innocence . . . such sweetness."

He glared at Rodin. "Then she retreated into a damn shell."

He made his way across the intervening space to the beechwood. Perhaps the head of a woman . . . the head bent, the eyes staring at nothing at all. A withdrawn woman. Beechwood had an undulating rhythm, and he'd be able to give it a silky finish. Sensuous. Yes, that would be perfect.

"Shells are built by people because of hurt," he murmured, gazing at the chunk of wood. "I sensed she was resisting remembering her past. Whatever it was that happened to her, it must have been awful.

"Aw, hell. What am I doing?" He started back across the room, but then he stopped and stood indecisively between the moody, turbulent elmwood and the beechwood that seemed to contain a woman who could bend a man's mind with her cool remote beauty.

"We made love," he murmured, "but in the end it didn't mean a thing. Not a damn thing."

Rodin opened his mouth and yawned.

Marissa stood outside the Whitmere Gallery, carrying on a lively conversation with herself. She was here simply out of curiosity, she told herself firmly. That was the *only* reason. And why on earth shouldn't she be curious? After all, she'd spent days alone with the man in his house. She'd fallen in love with the house he had built . . . and she'd fallen in love with him. Or thought she had.

But interest in his work was normal. If she hadn't met him, she would still want to see his work. Everyone did. With these assurances firmly in mind, she opened the door of the gallery and went in. Besides, talking to herself like this was an extremely bad sign.

"'May I help you?"

Marissa turned to find a distinguished, silver-haired man of perhaps fifty-five dressed in a gray pin-striped suit. "Yes, I called earlier about seeing Brady McCulloch's work."

"Oh, yes. You spoke with me. I'm Lawrence Whitmere, and you're Ms. Berryman."

"That's right."

He rubbed his hands together, obviously pleased. "As I told you over the phone, we consider ourselves very honored to have three McCulloch pieces. He doesn't conduct the business side of his work like most artists, you know. He doesn't accept commissions, and there are some years when he doesn't release any new work at all. When we heard that these pieces were available, we rolled up our sleeves and fought for them. I'm proud to say we won."

"May I see them?"

"Of course. Follow me." As he led her down the hall, he continued to chat. "You're one of the first to view them. We haven't even started taking bids yet. I think you'll agree that they're quite remarkable. One is in bronze; he did it about thirteen years ago, I believe. The other two are in wood."

They entered a well-lighted, spacious room. Three pieces stood on display platforms, each piece filled with life and movement.

A large magnificent bronze of three stags flying above the ground—their eyes wide, their ears stiff, their tails high—dominated the center of the room. The natural power and force of the animals had been captured forever for all to see. She circled the sculpture, running her hand lightly over their bronze coats, feeling the tendons that stood out in stark relief and the muscles that actually appeared to ripple. The mood was of strength and a joy of freedom. If she'd gone into the woods with Rodin, she might have seen these very stags.

"New York's Metropolitan Museum of Art is very interested in this one," Mr. Whitmere said.

She nodded and walked to the second piece.

"This is done in *lignum vitae*," Mr. Whitmere said, trailing after her. "It seems to be a favorite medium of McCulloch's."

Marissa silently marveled at the exquisite form of a mother bending over a sleeping child. Somehow Brady had taken a piece of wood and infused life and tender emotion into it. Without touching it, she moved on.

"You know, everyone was stunned when McCulloch withdrew to the Ozarks," Mr. Whitmere commented idly.

"Does anyone know why he did it?"

"Not really. He was one of the most feted young men in America, his work was becoming known worldwide, then . . ." He shrugged. "But now everyone agrees that his best work has been done during these last fifteen years."

The last piece was the smallest. It was of an old man, sitting on a porch, whittling, a look of intense satisfaction on his face.

How appropriate, she thought. Brady had been raised in the Ozarks, where wood craftsmen abounded. Perhaps as a little boy he'd watched an old man shaping an odd piece of wood into a dog or a deer. Perhaps this was Brady's tribute to his roots.

She spent a long time contemplating the old man and in the end decided it didn't matter what Brady McCulloch's intentions had been regarding this particular piece of sculpture. To her, it brought back the time she'd spent on a mountain with a man who had told her simply he worked with wood. It turned out he worked with wood like no one before him.

"I'd like to purchase this one," she said.

Mr. Whitmere's expression turned strained. "Oh, but I told you. We're not taking bids yet."

"I'll triple your minimum."

"Well . . ." He eyed the elegant young woman before him, a young woman he knew to be a cornerstone of Dallas society. Letting her have the work could be very good for his future business. He smiled. "As a personal favor to you, Ms. Berryman, I think we can make an exception."

At the luncheon she attended an hour later, she was asked to lead the program, discovered she hadn't a clue what the topic was, and bluffed her way through it. She picked at the chicken and said her good-byes as soon as possible.

She intended to go straight home and was surprised to find herself pulling her BMW 750iL to a stop in front of "Kathy's Crafts and Dec-orations."

As soon as she entered the store, she saw a young woman dressed in maternity jeans and a big oversized T-shirt with Robert Plant's face on the front and his concert tour dates on the back. The young woman pushed a mass of curly red hair behind her shoulders and came to-ward her. "Marissa, how wonderful to see you back."

"Hi, Kathy. I was hoping you'd be here." Marissa made her way through the yarns and silk flowers to the back of the store and its owner, Kathy Garth.

Kathy laid her hand on her burgeoning stom-ach and grimaced. "Paul will only let me spend a few hours a day here, now that our little one is on the way, but I don't mind. I have good help, and besides" —her emerald eyes twinkled merrily—"there's so much to do to get the new house ready for Paul Garth, Junior. I stay plenty busy."

Marissa's mouth dropped open. "A boy? You found out you're having a boy?"

Kathy nodded happily. "I had the test. Every-thing's fine, and now I know what color to make the nursery."

"Oh, Kathy, I'm so happy for you and Paul."

"We're pretty happy ourselves."

The beaming smile on Kathy's face revealed she had understated the case, and Marissa felt a pang of envy somewhere near her heart. "I need to call Paul."

Kathy changed gears from an expectant mother

to a concerned friend. "You most certainly do. When he read you'd been in an accident in Arkansas, he drove the police mad trying to get information. If you hadn't been in such an inaccessible area and the weather hadn't been so bad, he would have gone to you. Finally, though, the police were able to reassure him that you hadn't been hurt badly. Were they right?"

Marissa nodded and touched her forehead. "With makeup you can barely see the bruise."

"It sounds like it could have been so much worse. I can't even imagine how awful it must have been for you."

Marissa didn't want to talk to anyone about her accident, and the fact that she didn't, bothered her. It was as if those days spent with Brady were too painful . . . too glorious . . . to share with anyone. "Listen, Kathy, the reason I'm here is to see if you and Paul would like to come to dinner tomorrow night."

"Are you sure you're up to entertaining?"

"Positive."

"Well, then, we'd love to—Wait a minute. Tomorrow night's the scholarship benefit, isn't it?"

"Oh, you're right." Maybe she'd go. At least it would give her something to do. "Then how about the next night?"

"Sounds fine. I'll check Paul's calendar and get back to you." Kathy took a moment to study Marissa's black silk straight-skirted dress and green cashmere waist-length jacket. Black hose and black leather high heels rounded out the ensemble. Impulsively she said, "You look fabulous."

"I told you," Marissa said lightly, "it's makeup."

"I know better. Even with a flat stomach, I'll never be able to look like you. I've always admired your style."

"May I remind you that Paul married you, not me?"

A wide grin lit up Kathy's face. "That's true, thank heaven. At any rate, it's great to have you back."

Marissa smiled. "It's good to *be* back."

And it was, she assured herself minutes later, as she turned the car into the circular driveway of the home she'd bought after she'd divorced Kenneth Wrightman. This was where she belonged, she thought with satisfaction. All her friends were in Dallas. There was always something going on.

She brought the car to a stop in front of the house, pushed the gearshift to park, then froze at the sight of the man lounging casually on the front steps, his long jeans-clad legs stretched out in front of him.

Seven

Brady hoisted himself to his feet and ambled around the luxury car that didn't so much idle as purr. He pulled open the door and reached across her to switch off the key. Then he firmly grasped her arm and helped her out.

"Hello, Marissa. Nice car. Is this the replacement for the one that went into the river?"

She stared at him, her mouth open.

He grinned. "The way you drive, it might have been safer to have bought something a little less powerful."

"What are you doing here, Brady?"

"I'm happy to see you too." He lightly brushed a finger over the faint bruise on her forehead. "How are you? I'm fine by the way. Your Lillian couldn't understand why I didn't want to wait in the living room, but after I explained how good fresh air is for you, she went away and left me alone."

The afternoon breeze ruffled his dark brown hair. His steel-gray eyes bore into her with an intense mesmerizing quality. She glanced wildly around until she spotted his Jeep parked out on the street. How could she have missed it? "What are you doing here, Brady?"

"Why I've come to see you, Marissa, naturally." He took her arm again and began to guide her toward the house. "And I know that you're going to invite me in. Hospitality is everything in Texas, isn't it?"

Excitement and dread spurted through her, her emotions as tangled as her thoughts. She was just getting her life back together. Calling on friends, taking part in the activities of her many clubs and organizations, lining up engagements. This was her life, her *real* life.

She didn't want Brady here.

She'd bought his sculpture in a moment of weakness. Still, the idea of the constant reminder of Brady McCulloch in her home had been only slightly worrying, because the work had been carved out of a piece of wood and was an inanimate object. But the man beside her was warm-blooded, breathing, an extremely masculine man. Moreover a man to whom she'd made love with utter and total abandon.

As she inserted the key into the lock and opened the door, she bent her head to hide the flush that came up under her skin. That was the past, she told herself, trying to infuse strength into her legs and backbone. This was the present. She had her memory back now, and everything was going to be fine.

But moments later, watching him walk through the grand hall into the living room, she felt as if she'd loosed an elemental force into a refined setting. Destruction was imminent, she thought, then chided herself. Nonsense. She was in control. After all, *she* had left *him*.

Brady slipped his hands into the pockets of his jeans and gazed around the sumptuous elegance of the white room. "Quite a place you have here, Marissa, and you certainly don't have a problem with being crowded, do you? Of course, I can't imagine what you do with all these rooms."

While his attention was elsewhere, she studied him, trying to remember that once she had been reassured by this cold-eyed man. As big as the living room was, he dominated the area. As a matter of fact, looking at him, she decided he was the most formidable man she'd ever known. And when they'd made love . . .

Suddenly his head whipped around to her. "Where's Rodin?" she asked quickly, distressed that she'd been caught off guard.

"He's visiting his mother. I thought he'd be happier there."

Although there was no reproach in his voice, she saw her flawlessly decorated, immaculately clean home through his eyes and realized he was saying that the happy, eager-to-please, sometimes awkward Rodin would have no place here.

An inexplicable sadness crept over her as she thought of the hours Rodin had stayed by her side, comforting her with his undemanding presence.

Brady crossed to a table to pick up a slender Steuben glass vase. It looked like a cylinder of ice. He rolled it from one hand to the other, as if he were trying to melt it with his body heat.

If anyone else had handled the expensive vase so casually, she would have feared for its safety. But Brady had strong, sure hands. She'd trusted her body to them.

A tremble raced through her, and she wrapped her arms around her waist. "It didn't dawn on me who you were until I got back to Dallas."

He replaced the vase on the table and unleashed a hot glittering gaze on her. "You obviously felt you knew all you needed to: You made love with me. And despite what I said at the time about the men in your life, deep down I knew you weren't the promiscuous type. There's just something in those elegant bones of yours that strikes me as too fastidious. And now that I'm here in your home, I can see that I'm right."

With difficulty she controlled a tremor. "I meant that I didn't know you were the world-famous sculptor."

"You were disoriented the first couple of days. What was your reason after that?"

Her spine straightened. "Not everyone in the world knows who you are, Brady."

He closed the space between them until they

stood toe to toe. "No, but you would. Art would have played an important part in your education and background. And since you didn't make the connection, I can only conclude that it just wasn't important to you. You were at a place in your life when everything was stripped away except the essentials. Nice, wasn't it?"

He didn't attempt to touch her, but she felt compelled to step away from him. "Why are you here, Brady?"

"If I've kept an accurate count, you've asked me that question three times."

"Then tell me."

Shadows turned his face into a brooding mask. "You might say I was curious to see what it was you were in such a hurry to get back to. Since you said it wasn't a man, I'm wondering if it was this house. It looks like you, by the way. Like the person you are now, that is."

She stared icily back at him. "What do you want?"

He tilted his head to stare at her as if he couldn't believe she'd asked that. "I thought I just told you."

"No. There's something else."

He made a clicking sound with his tongue. "It's really sad for me to see how distrustful you've become."

"Brady, you haven't answered me."

"It's a very brave question, Marissa. Are you sure you're up to hearing the answer?"

"You're going to have to leave—"

"Ah, and that's not very brave of you at all.

But save your breath and your energy. I'm not leaving."

"Then, dammit, answer my question."

He smiled, pleased at her emotional outburst. "It's simple really. I've had second thoughts."

Her gaze became uncertain. "About what?"

"I helped you walk out of my life, Marissa. I took you into Samsonville, helped you rent a car, and watched you drive off. I lasted a week." He paused. "Since I don't see your bags packed and at the door ready for a trip to Arkansas, I gather you haven't had any problems adjusting to life without me."

"Are you saying you have?"

"I'm saying that I had sufficient problems to make me leave Rodin with his mother and come after you." He drove his hand through his hair, the first sign he'd given of less-than-perfect composure. "You and I were thrown together, Marissa, feelings developed and came to a head. Then you left. The way I see it, we didn't get a chance to see what would happen next."

She stood rooted to the spot, aware of the danger. Wordlessly she shook her head.

Before she realized his intentions, he had pulled her against him. "It's not over yet between us. Who knows? Maybe it'll never be over. Then again maybe it won't go any further. But either way I need to find out."

She swallowed hard and found it hurt. When she spoke, her words came out in a husky whisper. "What happened between us was my fault, Brady. I take total responsibility. I threw myself at you, and I know it."

"Yeah, you threw yourself at me—all one hundred and fifteen pounds of you. But I think I'm big enough and strong enough that I could have resisted if I'd wanted to. But I didn't, Marissa. I didn't want to."

Heaven help her, she thought, being this close to him was threatening to make her forget her convictions of right and wrong. Her gaze kept returning to his lips, and warmth had begun to curl inside her. She had to get him to leave. She moistened her bottom lip with her tongue. "Look, I'm sorry—"

His teeth came together with a snap. "Stop it. If it came down to it, I could apologize to you for taking advantage of you. But neither one of us can apologize away the effect we have on each other, and it would be a sin even to try."

Tearing away from him, she practically screamed at him. "It was only physical! Nothing more. But it was also perfectly understandable. I was weak. I'd been in an accident. You said it yourself, I was disoriented."

"The first couple of days. After that, you seemed to know pretty much what you were doing."

"I couldn't even remember who the hell I was, Brady!"

His eyes narrowed on her. Color was high in her cheeks, and her breathing had become uneven. He pressed his advantage. "So what you're saying is, now that you've regained your memory, you're not attracted to me. Is that right?"

"Yes, that's exactly right."

"I don't believe you."

With a few steps and a movement of his arms, she was against him again and he was kissing her just as if he'd never stopped.

She had her memory back, so she knew the danger of responding to him. But his kiss shook her all the way to her toes and she was helpless in the face of their mutual passion.

She put her arms tightly around his neck, and he deepened the kiss. At the same time, one hand slid upwards into her hair, his long fingers delving through the thick dark tresses, dislodging pins and undoing the sleekly elegant arrangement. His other hand cupped her bottom, lifting her slightly, so that she could feel his arousal. Weakness and heat suffused her body. She clung, not caring where he was taking her.

Her body remembered him so well. Her mind had never forgotten him. When he drew away, she felt momentarily bereft and found herself balancing unsteadily on her high heels, aware that his hand on her arm was her only stability. His husky laugh rippled along her nerves; gradually, painfully, her reason returned.

"So now we know that you're still attracted to me. The question is, what are you willing to do about it?"

She rubbed at her forehead with one finger. "Nothing. I'm not going to do a thing."

His thumb massaged her arm through the green cashmere. "I'm perfectly willing to keep kissing you until you give me the right answer, Marissa."

"The right answer in your opinion." She pulled away from him, more to prove to herself that she could than anything else. "What exactly is it that you want from me?"

He leaned his hips back against the top edge of a sofa and crossed his arms over his chest. His posture was relaxed, but there was nothing casual in the way he was looking at her. "Pure and simple, I want your time. I don't know if what's between us can grow outside the isolated atmosphere we were in last week, but I think we owe it to ourselves to give it a chance. And that, Marissa, means time spent together."

She shook her head. "No. If there is something between us—"

His short, derisive laugh cut her off. "*If?* Shall I kiss you again?"

She held up a hand. "Okay, there is something between us, but, Brady, it's only physical. If we leave it alone, it will die a natural death."

"And if we don't leave it alone?"

Her upper body was covered by cashmere, but she suddenly felt cold. "Then the attraction between us will run its course, and in the end we'll both be back where we started from, you on your mountain, me right here. It's just not worth it."

"Worth it? Most people would give years off their life to have just a portion of what we had that last afternoon and evening."

Color came up under her skin. "I've already apologized—"

"What the hell are you so afraid of?" He quickly crossed to her.

Her fingers curled into her hand until the nails cut the flesh of her palm. "I'm not afraid of anything."

"I don't believe you for a minute. From all appearances you have a very pretty life, but underneath all this, there's got to be something very ugly."

"You don't know what you're talking about."

"How many times did you tell me you didn't want to remember? How many times did you tell me you wanted to stay with me? Honey, you were running as hard as you could from something in your mind, and you latched onto me like I could save you. I want to know why."

"Why are you doing this?" she cried. "Why can't you just leave things alone?"

"Because I can't forget that when you opened your eyes and saw me, you said, 'Thank God I found you.' "

She stared at him, feeling as if she were balancing on a knife edge.

"Hello? Marissa?" CeCe called, her cheerful voice reaching them before she did. "Lillian said you were in here. I've been shopping, and I just had to show you the dress I found." She swept into the room, breezy and carefree and unaware of the charged atmosphere. Her eyes widened when she saw Brady. "Well, hello."

He smiled, banishing the intensity that had been etched in his face. "Hellooo."

"Marissa, I didn't know you had company."

Although her remarks were directed at Marissa, her eyes never left Brady.

Marissa slowly relaxed her hands. "That's all right. You didn't interrupt anything." She expected her remark to earn her a hard look from Brady, but he was still smiling at CeCe. She sighed. "CeCe, this is Brady McCulloch. Brady, this is CeCe Kavanaugh."

CeCe dropped her Neiman Marcus bag onto the floor. "*The* Brady McCulloch?"

Brady bent and picked up the bag and set it on the couch. "Well, I don't know. How many are there?"

"It is you. You're the one who saved Marissa, aren't you?"

His gaze sliced to Marissa, then back to CeCe. "That's debatable."

"Oh, but this is a great honor. Marissa, why didn't you tell me he was in town?"

"I didn't know until just a little while ago."

CeCe finally looked at Marissa. "Are you aware that your hair has come undone?"

"Uh . . ." She quickly touched her head, only now realizing what she must look like. She spotted a few hairpins on the floor and stooped to retrieve them.

"Are you staying here?" CeCe asked Brady.

Marissa forgot her hair and held her breath, fearful of what Brady would say.

"I have a suite at The Mansion," he said, naming the exclusive Dallas hotel that took luxury and individual attention to its guests to new heights.

CeCe hit her forehead with the flat of her hand. "Of course, I should have known you'd stay there. This is just so exciting. How long are you going to stay?"

He met Marissa's gaze. "I haven't decided yet."

"Then we must have a party for you. Right, Marissa?"

Marissa pressed a finger between her eyes. She was fast developing a headache, and she was wondering why in all these years she had never noticed how much her friend talked.

"I'm not much for parties," Brady said, watching Marissa.

CeCe's pretty face clouded with distress. "But you simply have to come to tomorrow night's benefit."

"I don't think—"

"No, you must. It's a dinner-auction, with the proceeds going toward art scholarships for gifted but disadvantaged students. And besides, Marissa needs an escort."

Marissa came to life. "CeCe, he said he's not much for parties, and I think we should respect that."

"'But—"

"And actually I'm afraid we're keeping Brady. He was just leaving when you came in."

"Oh, I'm sorry," CeCe said, crestfallen.

He took her hand between his and smiled charmingly at her. "Don't worry about it. But Marissa is right, I do have to be going."

Marissa blinked, surprised he had agreed with

her, then in the next moment started when he dropped CeCe's hand and reached for hers. "I'll see you tonight at eight, right?"

"Eight?"

"Where are you two going?" CeCe asked with interest, her happy nature restored.

"Dinner," Brady said.

"I don't think so—" Marissa began.

Her words were cut off by his mouth coming down on hers with gentle pressure.

"Eight," he whispered against her lips.

"Brady—"

"Don't bother showing me out. CeCe, I enjoyed meeting you. I know we'll see each other again. Good-bye."

Marissa watched him walk out of the room, her mind in a whirl.

CeCe had no such problem. She let out a whistle. "You didn't tell me the man was such a hunk. As a matter of fact, there seem to be a lot of things you failed to tell me."

She mentally shook herself, aware there was damage to control. "That's because there was and is nothing to tell."

"He kissed you, Marissa. He's taking you out to dinner tonight. He obviously came to town to see you. What more need I say?"

"Nothing. Okay? It's not what you think, and I want your promise that you won't mention to anyone that you met him here or even that he's in town."

"But why?"

"He's a very private person, and I'm sure he wouldn't appreciate your talking about him."

CeCe's face reflected the struggle going on inside her. She'd met a great artist no one had seen in years, and she wasn't going to be allowed to tell anyone. "Marissa . . ."

"CeCe!"

"Oh, all right," she said at last. "But do you think you could get him to bring you tomorrow night?"

"I'm sure he will have left town by then," she said firmly. "I wouldn't even be surprised if he cancels dinner tonight. You know how temperamental artists can be."

CeCe looked confused.

Marissa felt frightened. She'd had a reminder of how forceful and exciting Brady could be. Not that she'd really been able to forget. She'd wanted him desperately when she had amnesia. Now that she had her memory back, she wanted him just as desperately.

She'd counted on time and distance to shield her from him, and he was trying to remove both. If he came for her tonight, she wasn't sure she'd be able to resist him. There was only one thing she could do. As soon as she could get CeCe to leave, she would call The Mansion and tell Brady she had other plans for this evening. Then she would make sure that she did.

Marissa put a hand to her cheek. Why did she feel so warm, she wondered, getting up and opening the French doors that led from the bedroom out onto her terrace. She considered the terrace just one of the advantages of having her bedroom on the first floor and stubbornly refused to think of the empty second floor of the house.

On her way across the bedroom, she glanced at the clock. Seven-fifteen. Perfect, she thought. She was almost ready to go off alone to the movies.

She smoothed a damp palm down the side of her moonlight-colored silk and lace slip, the top of which formed a bra. Then slipping her stockinged feet into royal-blue suede high heels, she turned her attention to the clothes she had laid out on the bed. The violet silk blouse had a draped V neckline and one inner button closing, the royal-blue and violet print skirt was full and graceful, and the suede belt matched the shoes. She'd be overdressed for the movies, but the stylish clothes would provide her with armor for the upcoming evening alone.

She dressed quickly and sat down in front of the dressing table mirror, where she gathered the smooth shining length of her hair and began twisting it into the rope that she planned to entwine at the back of her head.

"Don't put it up," Brady said. "I like it better down."

She dropped her hands in stunned surprise and whirled around on the bench. "What are you doing here?"

"Lillian left me in the living room, but I decided I didn't want to wait in there. I'm sure she'll understand. She's growing used to me."

"I—I thought she'd left for the evening."

"I can understand your problem. This house is so big you don't know who's in it and who's not."

She glared at him suspiciously. "Didn't you get my message?"

"No, what message? By the way, I'm sorry I'm so early." With a sweeping glance, he took in her appearance. "You look lovely, but I think I like you best when you're wearing one of my flannel shirts."

She couldn't take her eyes off him. In his jeans, open-collared shirt, and denim jacket he was overpoweringly male. His virile presence in her bedroom brought a sexual tension to her that she wasn't sure she could fight. Then she focused with horror on what he carried in his arms—the sculpture she had bought that morning at the Whitmere Gallery.

He followed the direction of her gaze. "Lillian said it was delivered a short time ago. If you'd wanted one of my sculptures, all you had to do was ask, Marissa."

The sudden intimacy of his voice created havoc inside her, and words stuck in her throat.

"Lillian had placed it in the living room. Somehow it just didn't look right there. I thought I'd try it in here." He gazed around the white and lavender room. "I don't know though . . ."

She rose from her dressing table, feeling better able to confront him standing. "I'm sorry you don't like my home, but I've always been very comfortable here."

His dark brows rose as if she had surprised him. "And yet you didn't want to leave my home."

"I did, though, didn't I?"

His grin bared his white teeth. "Eventually."

Her hand briefly touched her forehead, then dropped to her side. "Just put the sculpture on the table there. I'll decide later where I want it to go."

He did as she said, staring thoughtfully at the piece for a moment before looking back at her. "You bought it at the Whitmere Gallery?"

She nodded.

"You must have paid quite a bit for it."

She folded her arms across her body. "I'm told that a McCulloch is better than money in the bank."

He ignored her comment. "Why this one, Marissa? Why 'The Whittler'?"

"It—it appealed to me."

"I would have thought 'Mother and Sleeping Child' would have been the one to appeal to a woman. This is a rougher piece. It's even a smaller piece. Not as showy."

Unwillingly she stared at the sculpture and was slowly drawn to its side. She lifted her hand and smoothed her fingers over the man's bent head, almost believing she could feel the crisp texture of his hair. "When I saw this, I thought of you growing up as a child in the Ozarks, watching men just like this one whittling. I thought of how they must have influenced you, and I thought of the generations to come whom you would influence."

He cupped her jaw and turned her face toward him. "Maybe," he said huskily, "you haven't changed after all."

For a moment she was caught by the warmth she saw glinting in his eyes. Then she remembered and stepped away.

"Let's go to dinner," he said. "We have a lot to talk about."

Eight

"You can order anything here from sirloin to waffles and everything in between," Brady told her as he slid in beside her, effectively but subtly trapping her in a corner booth of the restaurant to which he had brought her. "A bellman at The Mansion recommended this place after I told him what I was looking for—good food and privacy. Have you ever been here?"

"No, I haven't," Marissa said, glancing around the pleasant, dimly lit room, then reaching for the menu. She planned to order and eat fast. But the menu contained so many selections, it took her longer than she'd anticipated to choose. When she finally narrowed her choice to a chicken dish and laid aside the menu, she found Brady studying her.

"What are you going to have?" she asked to cover the awkwardness she felt.

"The lamb. Tell me, *can* you make waffles?"

Her mind went blank for a moment, then reluctantly she smiled. "No, I'm afraid not."

"Lillian cooks for you?"

She nodded. "And several other men and women before her. My father struck oil when he was a young man. Money poured in and so did everything that came with being an oil baron. My mother took to being a lady of leisure as if she were born to it. I *was* born to it. What's more, I was their only child."

"Ah, I get the picture. You were spoiled."

Her smile vanished. "In a nice, loving way."

He touched her hand. "You don't have to sound so defensive. I wasn't criticizing you."

"I wasn't being defensive."

"Sorry. My mistake. So tell me, are your parents still living?"

"No. They never seemed that close to each other as I was growing up, and they divorced when I was a teenager. That's why it seemed rather sad and ironic to me when they died within a week of each other."

"When was this?"

"Ten years ago. I was nineteen."

He let out a low whistle. "That must have been rough on you."

It was, she thought, but she'd had Kenneth to help her through it. And then he'd helped her through a good portion of her money. Thankfully, the waiter came up just then, and she was able to concentrate on giving him her order.

"Have you seen a doctor since you've been home?" Brady said after the waiter left.

She made a weary face. "I didn't see any sense in it, but, yes, I did."

"And?"

"And he ran tests, the results of which basically said I'm healthy and normal."

"That's good." He glanced away, then looked back at her as if he were uncertain. "There's something else I want to ask you."

She'd never seen him hesitant, and she became curious. "What's that?"

"It's about the men in your life . . ."

She sighed heavily. "I told you—"

"You said you weren't returning to anyone. Okay, fine. But what about someone in your past. Any serious love affairs or, for that matter, serious marriages?"

She stiffened. "What possible difference could it make?"

"There was someone, wasn't there?" he said, watching her closely. "What happened?"

She spread her hands out before her and tried to remain calm. "Just ordinary growing pains, Brady. I *was* married once. I met him during my first semester in college. My parents also met him and liked him very much. When they died, he was a great comfort to me. Several months later we married."

"How long did it last?"

"Three years. Then as I said, I grew up and matured and discovered I no longer needed someone to lean on."

He nodded his thanks to their waiter, who set a Scotch before him and white wine in front of Marissa. "Sounds real simple."

"It was."

"I don't buy it."

In the process of raising the wineglass to her lips, she jerked and sloshed some of the wine onto her hand. Carefully she set the glass down. "Brady, I came to dinner with you tonight because you're a stranger in town and deserved a return on the hospitality you gave me, but—"

"No, Marissa, that's not why you came to dinner with me tonight." He picked up her hand and ran his tongue across the wine-soaked skin.

Warmth flowed along her spine.

"You haven't come close to paying me back. As I recall, I let you sleep in my bed."

"Brady . . ."

"But we're not talking about that, are we?" he said smoothly, still holding her hand. "You see, Marissa, the truth is I'm absolutely fascinated by you. In the Ozarks, you were this amazingly sweet, utterly feminine, totally giving woman that drove me amed and eventually pushed all my hard-fought-for convictions right out of my head."

She moistened her bottom lip with her tongue. "Look, I don't think we should be talking about—"

"You can see where a man would have a hard time forgetting a woman like that, can't you, Marissa? So I decided to follow her—you—and what did I find? A very uptight, almost ice-encased woman who lives a sterile life all alone in a big house that's decorated with a bare minimum of the color and texture that you loved in my home. There's absolutely no identity in your house. I might not even have recognized you if it hadn't been for those eyes of yours, sweetheart."

His drawl of the word sweetheart was not quite affectionate, not quite sarcastic. She jerked her hand away. "That's not fair. You don't know enough about me to judge me."

"Then let me in on the things that make Marissa tick."

"No."

A candle flickered in the center of the table, spilling pale golden illumination over her white skin. Brady leaned back against the cushioned booth and sipped his Scotch. "I continue to be fascinated."

She heard her heart pounding and wondered when its rate had last been normal. "I'm surprised at you, Brady. You're a smart man, but you're missing something very simple here. There's no great mystery. I had amnesia, and now I don't. I'm my old self again."

"Are you? Then I guess when you were with me on my mountain, I was seeing you as no one's seen you in years. I feel very lucky."

Marissa reached for her wineglass.

"I got to see you with all shields down. But life, in the form of someone, must have hurt you terribly. You'd spent a lot of years practicing and assuming the protective coloration of the coolly sophisticated and untouchable young socialite. And once you regained your memory, it was automatic to assume it again, wasn't it?"

The waiter chose that moment to arrive with

their food, and Marissa's sigh of relief was almost audible. She stared blankly at the plate set before her, trying to remember what she'd ordered.

"What's wrong? Doesn't your chicken look good?"

Chicken! "I'm sure it's fine." She picked up her knife and fork and cut into the entree. Beside her, Brady did the same to his lamb. But when she swallowed, she found that the chicken stuck in her throat. She reached for her water glass and drank half of it down.

Brady pushed his plate back. "Funny. Ever since you left Arkansas, I haven't been able to work up any interest in food. How about you?"

"My appetite has been fine."

"I'm glad." He angled his body to face her, then lifted a hand to trace the line of her collarbone in the V of her blouse. "I want you to be well and happy. That's what I want for me too. I just want to see if we can be well and happy together."

"We can't, Brady." She was surprised to hear the break in her voice, and she cleared her throat. "It's not your fault, it's not mine. It's simply the way things are."

"And you'd like me to leave you alone."

"That's right."

He pressed a finger against her lips. "Not until I understand what made this shell."

She used anger to smother the flare of desire she felt. "Stop it. I'm twenty-nine years old. I'm bound to have a few rough edges."

"I didn't notice a single one when you were naked in my arms."

She steeled herself against the rush of heat the memory conjured, and turned on him. "What about you, Brady McCulloch? You talk about shells; you have a veritable concrete wall around you."

"You're absolutely right," he said softly. "But you burrowed right through it."

He was swamping her, and she could only shake her head.

"When you came into my life, Marissa, you were totally helpless. I found out that in order to help something helpless you have to open up a part of yourself that's vulnerable. And once that part of yourself is open, it's damn hard to close. It's why I'm here now. I figure that part of me will either open wider or it will close for good. It all depends on you."

Damn. Why were her eyes so moist? "You can't make me believe there is any part of you that is vulnerable."

"What would make you believe it?"

She stared broodingly at him. "Anytime anyone mentions your name, they talk about how fifteen years ago you disappeared into the Ozarks. What could possibly have gone so wrong to make you withdraw from the life that you were leading? Or will you tell me?"

He smiled gently. "I'll be glad to tell you, Marissa. All you had to do was ask."

Her heart gave a jolt. What in the world was she doing? She didn't need or want the further intimacy between them that would come if he shared a secret with her. She should tell him to forget it, that she wasn't interested. But she was.

"Fame came to me very young. I left home and went to New York City when I was twenty-one. I'd never seen a place that big or with that much energy. And I was the toast of the town. Hostesses begged me to come to their parties. Reporters fought for interviews. Critics called me a genius. Beautiful women called me sexy and fought to get into my bed. People bought my work. Everyone wanted something from me. I was getting rich; I was becoming a celebrity. It was heady stuff for a kid from the Ozarks.

"But I began to feel suffocated, and I didn't know why. I tried to spend more time in my studio, but you can only do so much work when you've had four hours sleep and you're hung over. So I'd put the work off until tomorrow and go out again."

"With another beautiful woman?" she asked, bothered at the pang of jealousy she felt.

"They were available. I was young."

"Of course," she said, infusing a coolness into her tone she wished were real.

"One morning I woke up, looked at what I'd been working on, and saw it was crap. That was when I realized that I'd become a celebrity instead of a sculptor. People were looking at me instead of my work. I was only twenty-four, but I knew if I kept going like I was, giving away pieces of myself like I'd been doing, I'd lose whatever talent God had given me. So I packed up and went home."

"To your mountain."

"To my mountain," he agreed, "and I haven't given an interview since, nor have I attended a party. But I've done damn fine work."

"Damn fine doesn't begin to describe your work, Brady."

"Thank you," he said softly. "There's something else I want you to know. I was never lonely on my mountain—not until you left it. I *had* to come after you."

Time stopped; candlelight melted over the two of them, creating a warmth and a bond. Marissa fought to escape the golden trap, but for the moment her faculties had deserted her.

"Wasn't your dinner satisfactory?" the waiter asked, peering inquisitively at their full plates, effectively breaking the spell.

"We don't know," Brady said, reaching into his pocket for his wallet. "We didn't eat."

"I'd be glad to bring you something else," the waiter said, trying to be helpful.

Brady counted out money to cover the check plus a generous tip and handed it to the young man. "Thanks. Another time."

The somewhat bewildered waiter took the money and departed.

Brady slid out of the booth, then reached back to help Marissa. When she was standing beside him, he said, "Now do you believe that I can be vulnerable?"

She searched for and located a new reservoir of strength within her. "I believe that from the time you were twenty-one until you were twenty-four you were vulnerable."

His mouth curved slowly upward. "You're a hard woman, Marissa Berryman. You may even begin to make me doubt the wisdom of coming after you."

"Good. Because you did the wrong thing, and I want you to realize it."

He dropped a quick kiss on her lips. "I'm sure your intentions are the best."

Marissa was silent on the drive back to her house. There was nothing she could say to him. He wanted to spend time with her, to see if what had developed during their time together would flourish and grow, or die.

She couldn't risk it. She didn't trust herself with him. But most of all she couldn't allow herself to trust him. Her emotions regarding him were in too much turmoil, her reactions to him too violent. Her life might be less than compelling from his viewpoint, but dammit, it was safe.

Everything in her was telling her to turn to him and pour out her heart to him. And after that to go into his arms and ask him to make love to her as he had their last night together. She ached for it.

But she'd fallen in love with Brady before she'd remembered why she couldn't love him.

And now she had to do everything she could to stem the tide of this love. To allow herself to trust and care for someone like Brady would be a totally self-destructive act. She simply wasn't brave enough.

He pulled into the circular drive and killed the engine. Before he could do or say anything, she opened the door, slid out, and shut the door after her. She leaned through the window, planning to say a civil good-night, but she felt his hands on her back.

"Looking for me?" he said softly, turning her to him.

"Only to say good-night." She slipped away and managed to get up the porch steps before she felt his hand grasp her arm.

"Why do I think you're not planning to invite me in?"

She gazed up at him. He was a larger-than-life person, a brilliant artist who sculpted works that moved people with their exquisite beauty. He was also a potently virile man who had had her begging him to make love to her. And then he had done so, amazingly, unforgettably.

At times she felt that fighting him was as impossible as climbing up a mountain. But she'd done just that, she reminded herself. She would extricate herself from this involvement with him too.

"Inviting you in would serve no purpose."

His eyes glinted with steel-like determination. He curved his hand beneath her hair to take hold of her neck. "From your viewpoint, maybe. But an invitation would make me extremely happy."

"No, Brady," she whispered. "No."

"Remember when you pleaded with me to say yes?" He took a step forward, forcing her to step backward until she came up against one of the granite columns that supported the porch. "Remember when we made love standing in the shower?" he said, pressing his body into hers. "I've never wanted anyone so much in my life. I couldn't get enough of you."

"Brady—"

"Shhh. Just remember . . . remember how it felt to be together." He kissed the side of her mouth, then darted his tongue along her lips.

His lower body ground against her, and the feel of his arousal sent flames licking through her bloodstream. "Brady, please, don't!"

He skimmed his hand down her side, over the curving lines of her hip and down to her thigh; then he inched her skirt upwards until he could slip his hand between her legs.

Her head went back against the column and she gasped.

Caressing the soft bare skin above the line of her stockings, he kissed the arching curve of her neck. "Say yes to me, Marissa, like you did on the mountain. I've been a week without you, and I need you so badly."

Sensual abandon threatened. She rolled her head back and forth, but the thing she was trying to escape was inside her. His lips kept up their assault on her. And his hand . . . she felt it slide beneath the lace edge of her panties, and to her horror her hips rose, meeting his fingers.

She pushed against his shoulders, but in her weakened condition, she had no effect on him. And it felt so good to have him touching her, kissing her—No!

"'I've been through hell since you left," he murmured hoarsely, kissing and nipping at her lips. "You set me on fire and then you left. That fire's been burning ever since, and it won't go out. Help me, Marissa. Help me."

A broken sound escaped from her. "It's only physical. That's all." She opened her mouth and parted her legs a little wider.

"With us that could be enough."

His fingers stroked sensitive nerves to full life. The hands that were pushing against him now clutched at his jacket. "No."

"I'm going to make love to you now," he muttered, his words an agonized growl. "Right here. I have to."

"But it won't mean anything."

"It will mean everything." He groaned. "The pain is excruciating. It's got to be for you too."

"No."

"I could be inside you before you draw your next breath, Marissa. But I want to hear you say yes." He felt her tense, felt her lift her knee and rest the sole of her high-heeled shoe behind her against the column. Understanding what was happening, he gently massaged the tiny bud that nestled so sweetly within the folds of her femininity.

"You would have made love in the mud. We did make love standing in the shower, then on the rug. Do you remember how much you wanted me then? You still do. Inside, you haven't changed completely. I saw it when you looked at my sculpture. You're halfway between what you've taught yourself to be and what you were with me. Come back to me. We can make love right now against this column. Do you have any idea how wonderful it would feel?"

She grabbed at his shoulders as a wave of pleasure slammed through her, then subsided, only to begin to rise again. "Let me go," she cried, the words automatic and rapidly losing their meaning.

His fingers kept up the movement. "I can make that happen again and again . . . all night long, in fact, . . . but it's not going to be enough. You want *me*, Marissa. All you have to do is admit it."

Tears slid down her cheeks. "No . . . no . . ."

Before she was really ready, he eased his hand from her and stepped jerkily away. Ragged tearing sounds came from his throat. His face was twisted with a torment she felt inside herself. At first she didn't think she'd be able to stand. But it was important that she get away from him.

She found her balance and edged past him. But as her aching breasts accidently brushed against his chest, her eyes closed and she went still. He had left her as she was climbing toward another peak; she felt ill, an internal pressure simmering wildly.

"Marissa . . ."

He spoke her name as if she could give him life.

She shook her head. No. No.

At the front door, her hand shook so badly, she could barely unlock the door. Inserting the key took her three times as long as usual, and all the while she was aware of him standing behind her, a powerful force pulling at her.

At last she was in the house, and she shoved the door closed without daring to give him a last look. She concentrated on not collapsing, on putting one foot in front of the other, on making her way through the house to the sanctuary of her bedroom.

Once there, she switched on the light and walked to the center of the room. Her muscles were quivering; her nerves were pulsating with unfulfilled demands. The air around her was charged with an electricity that burned along the surface of her skin. She was being pulled apart, and she doubted there was any saving her. Slowly she raised her head and looked toward the French doors.

He was there on the terrace.

He was just staring at her. That was all. Just staring. But the intensity of his passion reached across the distance and assaulted her.

She had no choice. Holding his gaze, she began to undress.

She unbuckled the brass buckle of the belt and released it. The strip of royal-blue suede dropped to the floor. He didn't move.

She unfastened the skirt. The blue and violet print fluttered to the carpet. She stepped out of it. His gaze didn't falter.

She undid the inner button of the violet blouse and let it slide down and off her arms. The terrace doors were shut, and it was autumn, but she felt buffeted by a strong, hot wind.

The moonlight-colored silk slip was skimmed

over her head and tossed away. And finally she was left wearing only her silk panties, lace garter belt, royal-blue stockings, and high-heeled suede shoes. Urgency whipped at her, pulling her.

She walked toward him, grasped the two handles, and opened the doors outward.

"Yes," she said.

Still he didn't move.

The cool night air flowed over her. She shivered, on fire. Without doing a thing, he drew her to him.

She went. She didn't want him, couldn't love him, but she had to have him. She worked at the buttons of his shirt until she could slide the flat of her hands inside and the dark soft hairs curled sensuously around her fingers. He trembled; something heavy bound her chest tighter and tighter. If he didn't make love to her soon she might die.

She stood on tiptoe and placed a kiss at the corner of his mouth. "Yes," she said again. "Yes, Brady. Please."

With a blurringly fast motion that made her dizzy, he scooped her into his arms and carried her inside to the bed.

Within moments his clothes and the remainder of hers were discarded and he was positioning himself above her, supporting himself with his arms. The muscles of his body quivered with anticipation. The throbbing pain deep inside him grew. "Never again say no to me . . . at least not tonight."

Her eyelids were heavy with desire. She could barely see him. "Yes."

He thrust into her with all the power that was in him. His hips rocked with a primitive rhythm. Ecstasy burst within her.

The moon rose in the sky, spilling silvery light through the terrace doors and onto the bed. And all through the night, she didn't tell him no. Not once.

Nine

Marissa opened her eyes and peered at the bedside clock. Eleven-thirty. From the light that filled the room, she guessed in a vaguely disinterested way that it was now morning.

Her lips curved into a private smile. What a night she and Brady had shared. Contentment permeated each and every bone in her body. Their passion had burned brightly through the night. They'd resisted sleep, choosing instead to concentrate on the pleasures that seemed infinite. Finally, totally exhausted, they had fallen asleep in each other's arms.

Stretching lazily, she felt desire begin to reassert itself. "Brady?" She rolled over and faced an expanse of empty bed.

Bewildered, she sat up and gazed around the room. There was no sign of him or his clothes. The sunlight that flooded through the open drapes of the French doors highlighted the fact that she was alone in the room; she narrowed her eyes against the glare.

Disappointment and a mounting tension cut through the hazy glow of contentment she had been feeling, and reluctantly she braced herself to deal with reality. She pushed her hair away from her face and propped herself up against the pillows, thinking that she would have laughed if she hadn't wanted so much to cry.

She had no idea why Brady had stolen out of her bed and left without saying good-bye, and she supposed in the long run the reason didn't really matter. Last night she'd been swept away by passion, but the light of day clearly illuminated her mistake. And it had been *her* mistake. There was no way she could blame Brady. He had been tenacious and dogged in his pursuit of her, but she should have been stronger. After all, she was the one who knew the price of loving to the point where judgment became clouded. And the price had always been more than she could afford.

The phone rang. With a weariness that had nothing to do with lack of sleep, she reached for it. "Hello."

"Sounds like you just woke up."

She'd never talked on the phone with Brady, but his deep voice was unmistakable. As was the quickening of her pulse. From this moment on, she vowed, she would be in complete control. "Hello, Brady."

"I'm sorry I'm not there. But if it's any consolation, getting out of your bed and leaving you wasn't easy, believe me."

She carried on a quick fight with herself and lost, as curiosity got the better of her. "Where did you go?"

"My agent had made an appointment with me for this morning. We met for breakfast at The Mansion."

"Does your agent live here?"

"She lives in New York, and she's a diehard city person. Since I hardly ever leave Arkansas and she hates to come to 'the wilds,' as she calls the mountain, it's real hard on her. She saw my trip here as an event and seized the opportunity to meet with me. I'm fully aware that representing me isn't easy at best, so I decided the least I could do was show up." His voice changed timbre. "I did it reluctantly, though. Somehow you manage to be desirable even asleep."

She bent her head and rubbed a finger over the center of her forehead. "'Brady, about last night . . ."

"Uh-oh."

"I want you to know that I don't blame any-one but myself—"

"Blame?"

"It can't happen again."

"Boy, I can't leave you alone for a minute, can I?"

She exhaled a pent-up breath. "Look, Brady. It's just as well you called instead of coming back over. Seeing each other again would only be painful for both of us and wouldn't accomplish anything. We need to call it quits right now before anything else happens."

Silence that crackled like electricity surged through the line to her.

"Over before it really starts, huh? How very neat, Marissa. How cut and dried. How bloodless."

She closed her eyes. "I know you don't understand, and I'm sorry that I can't explain. But take my word for it, this is the best way. Go back to your mountain, Brady. Create beautiful things. And forget me. Time will make it easy, you'll see."

"I like things easy," he said in a soft, deadly drawl, "but, honey, nothing about you and me has been easy, and I don't see it starting to be now."

"Good-bye, Brady." She hung up the phone before she could change her mind and slid down into the bed, pulling the covers over her.

She felt like she was clinging by her fingernails to the ledge of a high, rocky cliff and consequently to life. The belief that she'd done the right thing sustained her, but it didn't stop the ripping, cutting pain that threatened the wholeness of her already bleeding heart.

Eventually she forced herself out of bed and into the shower. She pushed the memory of that other shower out of her mind and turned the water to as cold as she could stand. Minutes later, fortified, she wrapped herself in a big terry-cloth robe and returned to her bedroom.

She wasn't surprised to see CeCe sitting by the French doors, having a cup of coffee. They'd been in and out of each other's homes since they were girls.

"Good afternoon," CeCe said. "You're getting a late start today. Aren't you feeling well?"

Marissa crossed to the silver coffee service laid out on a low table and poured hot steaming coffee into the second cup. After her first taste of the delicious brew, she decided to give Lillian a raise. "I just felt like a lazy morning. What are you up to?"

"I had to have some last-minute alterations done on the dress I'm wearing tonight, and I was out picking it up." CeCe's eyes sparkled. "Wait until you see it."

"Wasn't I with you when you bought it?" she asked, puzzled. She couldn't imagine CeCe buying something without her. The two of them always shopped together, and they did a lot of shopping.

"You were in Arkansas."

"Oh."

"At the time, we didn't think you'd be back for tonight. Remember?"

Marissa sank onto the love seat across from CeCe. "That's right." She sipped the coffee, hoping her brain would click into gear soon. Her life before her trip—the social obligations and the effort she'd always put into being dressed to the nines—seemed so long ago, but in reality it had been less than two weeks.

"Who are you going with tonight?" CeCe asked in a conspiratorial tone.

She knew what CeCe was asking, but delayed her answer as she suddenly caught a glimpse of her life in the years ahead. A succession of luncheons, dinner parties, committees, and clubs stretched endlessly before her like a long hollow tunnel. CeCe's enthusiasm for her life was to be envied, she decided. "I'm not going with anyone," she said. "I haven't seen or talked to many people since I've been back, you know."

"Come on!" CeCe set down the coffee cup with an abruptness that splashed coffee onto the china saucer. "What about Brady McCulloch? I was certain you'd be attending with him."

"No." She tried to imbue her shrug with nonchalance. "He's returned to Arkansas."

"That's too bad," CeCe said, clearly disappointed. "But, Marissa, there are any number of men who would love to take you. Just pick up the phone."

"I'm not even sure I'll go."

"But you've got to. I mean, not going because you're not here is one thing. But you're *here*, so you've got to attend."

Marissa struggled with CeCe's logic, and decided it would have made sense two weeks ago. "Who are you going with?"

"Edward McCarthy. The only thing is, Jane is sick, so I'm pitching in to help make sure the auction items are organized, and I have to go early. I told him I'd drive my own car and meet him there." CeCe smiled with a sudden thought. "Why don't I come by and pick you up? We could use your help."

"I don't think so, CeCe."

"But you are coming, right? You know you don't have to have an escort."

"I know, and . . . I'll see."

CeCe gazed at her thoughtfully. "You've changed since you've come back. I can't put my finger on how."

Marissa shook her head. "I don't think I've changed at all. There are times I wish I had, though. Now tell me, what else do you have lined up for this afternoon?"

"I have an appointment to have my hair done." She glanced at her watch. "Oops. I'd better get going." She jumped up, then paused and gazed at Marissa. "You know, don't you, that if you're having any kind of problem, I'm here for you?"

"I do know, CeCe," Marissa murmured, touched, "and thank you."

The afternoon seemed endless to Marissa. She had nothing to do, and none of her usual activities appealed to her. She considered shopping, but she couldn't think of a thing she needed.

She didn't hear from Brady.

She spent time at her desk scrutinizing her calendar for the coming months and checking the files she kept on the various charities for which she worked. Everything was in perfect order.

And she didn't hear from Brady.

She thought about going to the beauty salon to have her hair and nails done, but she decided she didn't want to be around people. In the end, she gave herself a manicure and washed her hair and came to the conclusion that she was lonely.

She was glad that Brady had taken her advice and gone home.

The dinner-auction that evening began to have more appeal for her, especially when she considered the alternative of staying home alone with her thoughts.

She decided to wear something bright and drop-dead sophisticated, something that would make her feel like her old self again. After an exhaustive search of her closets, she found just the right evening gown.

The dress was a tight-fitting sheath of red ruched silk crepe, cut low, with off-the-shoulder small sleeves, and it followed the curves of her body to below the knees where it flowed outward to the floor. Best of all, to her mind, a train cascaded from the back and trailed dramatically behind her. The dress definitely fit the bill.

She twined her dark hair into an elegant configuration at the base of her neck, fastened large triangular red stone earrings to her ears, donned red satin high-heeled shoes, and pronounced herself ready to face the world. With her favorite perfume wafting around her, she turned out the bedroom light and walked through the darkened empty house to the front door.

She checked her evening bag for her car keys, opened the door, and stepped outside. And stopped. Brady was there, one elbow propped on the hood of his Jeep.

His gray eyes swept over her. "I seem to remember saying once that you wear clothes well, no matter what they are or how many there are." He pushed away from the Jeep and ambled up the steps to her, power in every move he made. "Actually, you take my breath away, no matter what you wear, but this dress is—is—" He frowned. "Bare. Why don't you have a coat on?"

"I . . ." She glanced down at herself. "I guess I wasn't thinking. I'll go back in and get something in a minute. Brady, I thought you'd gone back to Arkansas."

"Did you?" He bent his head and pressed his lips to the side of her neck. "Mmm. You smell good. What is the name of that perfume?"

Her heart began to pound as it always did when he came near. "Never mind. Brady, I'm on my way out for the evening."

"I know. You're going to some sort of charity thing. I'm here to take you."

"Take me? But you can't!"

"Why not? Your friend CeCe invited me. She also said you needed an escort."

Her teeth snapped together. "She was wrong. Brady, I tried to make myself as clear as I could today on the phone, but—"

He took her arms and pulled her against him with such force she was momentarily without breath.

"Don't worry your beautiful head about it. You made yourself crystal clear. I just don't accept what you said, at least not yet." He didn't give her a chance to protest, but went on in a hard, uncompromising voice. "I've called myself every kind of fool. Part of me says run like hell back to the mountain and forget I ever pulled a halfdrowned woman in from the storm. But there are parts of me, Marissa, that say stay, figure her out." His grip on her arms tightened. "Parts that say no other woman has ever been able to make me feel the things that she does. And then I call myself a fool again. But for now at least it doesn't seem to matter. I'm here. I'm staying. Just accept it, because short of calling the law, there's nothing you can do about it." His gaze sharpened. "The ball's in your court, sweetheart. Are you going to call the police?"

If she'd been hit on the head, she couldn't have felt any more stunned. "No, I . . ."

"Good." He released her, whipped off his denim jacket, and settled it around her shoulders. "There. You'll create a new fashion trend, and you won't need to go back into the house." He reached behind her and pulled the door closed with a click, then checked to make sure it had locked. "Where are we going, by the way?"

He had her halfway to the Jeep before she came to her senses. "Wait a minute." She stopped, her social training coming to the fore with a vengeance. He was wearing his usual attire of jeans, an open-necked dark blue shirt, and boots. There was no doubt that he was a ruggedly attractive, incredibly sexy man who had the power to make her knees go weak. And she was positive that there wasn't a woman in the world who wouldn't agree with her. But he wasn't dressed correctly to attend this party tonight. "You can't go like that," she said definitely. "It's a black-tie affair."

An unexpected twinkle sprang into his eyes, catching her off guard.

"You don't think I'd be welcome dressed as I am?"

"It's just that . . . you'll be out of place."

"You think they'll ask me to leave?"

"They . . ." She briefly closed her eyes and shook her head. Good heavens, what was she thinking about? She grinned, unable to believe how stupid she'd been. She couldn't imagine a host or hostess anywhere not absolutely thrilled to have Brady McCulloch as a guest under any circumstances. "Just forget I said that. Okay?"

He returned her grin. "Okay."

As more and more people clustered around Brady, Marissa was pushed farther and farther away until he reached his long arm through the crowd, grasped her hand, and brought her back to his side.

"It's a great honor to have you with us tonight, Mr. McCulloch," one Dallas matron said, nearly beside herself at the idea of the prestige he lent to the affair.

"Brady, please," he said charmingly.

"I invited him," CeCe said, pleased with herself and looking lovely in a glittering black dress.

"If we'd only known, we could have arranged a tribute," the matron said.

"I'd much rather be just a guest, I can assure you."

A reporter there to cover the social event shouldered her way through the crowd. "Mr. Mc-

Culloch, no one can remember the last time you were seen in public. Is there a special reason why you're here tonight?"

"As a matter of fact, there is." Marissa went still, and Brady squeezed her hand reassuringly. "I consider supporting gifted but disadvantaged students a very special reason."

"Yes, of course." Excitement heightened the color in the reporter's cheeks, and the hold on her tape recorder tightened. She had the potential for a *real* story for a change. "But could you tell me a little bit about why you disappeared fifteen years ago? My readers would be extremely interested."

He looked faintly amused. "Fifteen years ago is in the past. I'm sure your readers are too sensitive and too intelligent to want to probe into something that was a personal decision."

Some of the color faded from her cheeks. "Then could you perhaps tell me about your works-in-progress?"

He smiled at her. "I never discuss works-in-progress."

"I see." The rest of her color drained away. "I don't suppose you'd care to comment on whether you're planning to move to Dallas?"

"Dallas is a lovely city. Anyone would enjoy living here."

A tall good-looking man shouldered his way through the crowd. "Excuse me, everyone. Excuse me. It's time to be seated. Excuse me, but they're asking everyone to find their tables now. Thank you. Thank you." By the time he reached Brady and Marissa, the crowd around them was slowly dispersing. Grinning, he extended his hand to the other man. "I'm Paul Garth, a friend of Marissa's, and it's a pleasure to meet you."

'It's nice to meet a friend of Marissa's," Brady said, shaking hands.

"Hello, Marissa," Paul said.

"Hello." She mouthed the word thanks.

"You've pulled off quite a social coup by bringing Brady."

"Actually, Paul, he brought me."

"Ah." He gazed back at Brady. "I gather I can thank you for saving Marissa's life."

Brady hesitated, but Marissa said, "You knew, Paul?"

"Not until I saw him with you here tonight, but I can add two and two quite well."

"Well, keep it to yourself," she muttered.

Paul smiled at Brady. "Great. Blackmail material. Would you two like to sit at my table tonight? Kathy would love to meet you."

"Kathy is Paul's wife," Marissa explained, at the same time craning her neck to get a better view of the huge hotel ballroom. "Where's CeCe? I'm sure she expects us to sit at her table. She's taking credit for Brady's being here, you know. The more she tells the story, the more elaborate it becomes. I fully expect by evening's end to hear that she personally went to Arkansas, threw him bodily into her car, and brought him back here."

Paul joined Brady in laughter, then said, "That's CeCe for you. And as for where she is, I think I saw her heading off to comfort the reporter. You're a brutal interview, Brady."

"I thought his answers were perfect," Marissa said.

Brady stared at her.

Paul cleared his throat. "Have we made a decision on the table yet? CeCe and her date can join us at our table if it comes to that."

Brady looked to Marissa for the decision.

"We'd love to sit at your table, Paul. Thanks for asking. Oh, there's Mr. Whitmere. From the look of it, Brady, he wants to meet you."

He followed the direction of her gaze with sharp interest. "Of the Whitmere Gallery?"

She nodded.

"Then by all means, let's go over. Paul, we'll join you in a minute."

Marissa led Brady to the side of the room where Mr. Whitmere was practically dancing in anticipation, and performed the introductions.

"Ms. Berryman, you didn't tell me you actually *knew* Mr. McCulloch. This is such an honor, I can't tell you. Mr. McCulloch, I'm not sure if you're aware of it, but we have two of your pieces—we had three, but I was delighted to sell Ms. Berryman 'The Whittler.' And the interest that has been generated, well . . . And now having you in town and meeting you—"

Brady cut in. "You have the 'Three Stags' and 'Mother and Sleeping Child,' is that right?"

Mr. Whitmere nodded. "Exquisite, powerful." He shook his head, overcome. "You are truly a great—"

"I'd like to work a deal with you, Mr. Whitmere.

If you'll send for 'Mother and Sleeping Child' and have it brought here before the auction starts, I'll replace it with two other works."

Mr. Whitmere stared at him, astounded. "You want me to what?"

"I'd like to donate the piece to the auction tonight."

"Are you aware of what that piece is worth?" Mr. Whitmere asked, incredulous.

Brady's lips quirked. "I'm *well* aware, I assure you."

"I don't know . . . . Uh, two other pieces, did you say?"

"That's right, and I assure you, they're pieces that are of equal or greater importance and value. And of course you would be doing me a huge personal favor. I would be in your debt."

Mr. Whitmere pulled himself together very fast. "I'll send for the piece right away. Lord, I can't believe a McCulloch is going to be auctioned off tonight." He turned and started off, talking to himself. "Wait until the crowd learns about this. They're going to go wild."

Marissa turned to Brady. "Are you sure you want to do this?"

He grinned. "Not you too?"

His gray eyes were beautiful when they contained laughter, she discovered. She sighed. He could defeat her so easily if she allowed it. She drew a cloak of formality around her. "Your donation is going to mean a great deal to the scholarship fund, Brady. Thank you."

He raised her hand and kissed the back of it.

"Thank you for allowing me to be your escort tonight."

Her lips drew together in a firm line. "Allowing? Did I miss something?"

He smiled. "I could stand here all night looking at you. You're incredibly beautiful."

She turned her head to view the crowd. "I think they're about to start serving. We should find Paul's table."

"Whatever you say, Ms. Berryman."

"Brady . . ."

For the last few minutes, he'd watched a variety of different emotions play over her face. Now her expression was troubled. "What?" he asked softly.

"I thought you controlled the interview with great finesse, but you hated it, didn't you?"

"Every second of it."

"You realize, don't you, that she was a society reporter? If you stay in town, there'll be others who won't back off so easily."

"I can handle it. I'm a different person than I was fifteen years ago. I'm more balanced, more grounded."

"You told CeCe you didn't like parties."

"I don't, especially large events like this. And I hate publicity and having my picture taken. I understand why primitive people feel that cameras can steal their souls. But I also understand that I can't always avoid that sort of thing."

"You handled it with grace."

"I wasn't sure I would, you know. When the

crowd first started forming around us, I got a flash of *déjà vu* that wasn't pleasant."

"It didn't show."

He put his hand on her bare shoulder and softly caressed the silky skin. "I wanted to be here with you so badly I was determined to deal with and overcome anything."

She stiffened, sensing he was trying to make a point she wasn't going to like. "But it turned out it wasn't so bad for you after all. You've done just fine."

"Because I was willing to put the past behind me. You can too. Whatever it is, Marissa."

"That's not fair," she whispered.

"I haven't even started yet."

Ten

During dinner, Brady held court like some savage prince, drawing people into the seductive circle of his charm. Marissa viewed him warily. She'd known his kindness and concern. She'd known his potent masculinity and virile sexuality. But he'd never shown her this roughhewn, magnetic charm, and she didn't trust it or him.

At the start of the auction, it was announced that the McCulloch sculpture, "Mother and Sleeping Child," would be auctioned at the end of the evening. The excitement began to build.

And Brady turned his attention to her. "Tell me when you see something you like," he said, his voice pitched low just for her hearing, "and I'll get it for you."

She cast an idle glance at the fur coat currently being shown on the stage. "I don't think so."

"What are you turning down? The fur coat or my offer to buy you something?"

"Both."

He looked around the room at people who could afford to purchase ten such coats if they so chose but who were eagerly bidding. "It's for a good cause, Marissa."

"I'll send them a check."

"Oooh, *cold*. Cold. No wonder they call you the Ice Queen of Dallas Society. When you really try, you can make that shell of yours impenetrable. At the moment I don't think I could get through to you with a hatchet."

Cool amethyst eyes turned on him. "Then don't try."

"How about a face-lift?"

She blinked. "I beg your pardon?"

"A face-lift. The fur coat went to that couple at table twenty-five, and now they're auctioning off a face-lift. You never know, Marissa. A few years down the road you might wish you'd let me bid on this for you."

Under any other circumstances, she would have laughed. But he was doing a remarkable job of keeping her off balance, and she could feel her nerves tightening. She took a healthy gulp of wine. "I'll chance it."

Item after item went on the auction block and was sold to the satisfaction of both the purchaser and the scholarship committee. Brady kept up a running commentary. Marissa did her best not to rise to his bait. But when she heard him give a low whistle, she couldn't help asking, "What is it?"

"The auctioneer's assistant just brought out a necklace that would go perfectly with your dress."

Curious, Marissa looked up at the stage. The bib-style necklace was wrought in beaten gold and had a single ruby at its center. She was interested in spite of herself. "It is very unusual."

"Unusual? It's pagan. You're going to have it." He raised his hand, jumping into the bidding.

"What are you doing?" she hissed.

He leaned toward her and spoke low so that the other people at the table wouldn't be able to hear. "I told you. I'm going to purchase the necklace for you, but not because it will complement your dress."

Control of the evening had disappeared when she'd opened the front door and seen him leaning against his Jeep. She waited with fascinated dread to see what he would say next.

"The necklace reminds me of the jewelry the women of ancient Crete wore. The climate was warm, and they wore form-fitting dresses of fine sheer cloth that started at the waist." He kept track of the bidding and raised his hand again at the appropriate moment. But the spotlight of his attention on Marissa never wavered for more than a moment. "They considered bare breasts a sign of womanly beauty, and they darkened their nipples with a compound made of the juices of crushed berries and fragrant oils." He paused to calmly indicate he would raise the current bid, then went on. "I always wondered if they did it to enhance the color of their nipples or to invite a taste from their lover. What do you think?"

She didn't want the heat that was invading her body. She didn't want to be enticed by his words. "Brady—"

He gave the auctioneer another signal, and Marissa's head felt as if she'd drunk too much wine. The price for the necklace climbed as the bidding narrowed to Brady and one other man, and he continued whispering in her ear.

"Of course, you can drive me crazy without doing either. When you walked toward me last night wearing only high heels, stockings, panties, and the garter belt, your breasts swayed ever so gently . . . your nipples pointed . . ." He raised his head. "I've won."

"Congratulations, Brady," Paul said from across the table.

"Congratulations," someone else said.

"Marissa, you're so lucky," CeCe said, beaming.

"CeCe!"

"Oh, I'm sorry. I just naturally assumed—"

"You assumed right," Brady said. "The necklace is going to look beautiful on Marissa. As a matter of fact, I can hardly wait to have a private viewing."

Kathy gazed from one to the other, sensing the undercurrents and wanting to smooth things over. "It will look perfect with your dress, Marissa."

"I've never thought this dress needed a necklace," she said, her voice husky.

"Maybe you're right," Brady said, studying

her low neckline with consideration. "We'll forget the dress then. Excuse me while I go make arrangements for payment."

The evening was almost over, Marissa told herself with equal parts of thankfulness and relief. She plastered a smile on her face and vowed not to let it slip.

When Brady came back to the table, he had a black jewelry case with him, the necklace nestling inside. While the case was passed around the table, he leaned over to her. "They offered to deliver it tomorrow, but I wanted it for tonight."

She'd tried to be so strong all evening, Marissa thought, but he was bombarding her just as the storm had done, and she wasn't sure how much more she could stand. The noise of the room seemed to rise to a cacophony. The people began to recede.

"Brady, your sculpture is next," CeCe announced.

Marissa saw Kathy turn to Paul. "I would love to have it. Do you think the price will go too high?"

Paul smiled tenderly at his lovely young wife and lightly laid his hand on her rounded stomach, where their child grew. "The price will be astronomical, but you and our baby are going to have it."

Delicate color came up in Kathy's cheeks as she gazed at Paul with adoration and trust.

Marissa's field of vision narrowed to Paul and Kathy and the sculpture behind them on the stage, and she felt a jolt of pain that took her breath away. Like something so cold inside her it burned.

But why did it hurt now? she wondered. She'd observed Kathy's radiance over the months. She'd seen Paul doting over her, beside himself with joy at the idea of being a father. And just a day or two ago, she'd viewed the exquisite wooden sculpture that represented such deep tenderness and love.

But now seeing the two together was suddenly too much for her to bear.

She felt Brady touch her. "What's wrong, Marissa?"

"Nothing." The taste of the word was bitter in her mouth. Nothing. That summed up so perfectly what Kenneth had left her.

"You've gone white."

Alarm bells went off, adrenaline surged. She mustn't let him believe that there was anything wrong. The long-time practice of covering up her feelings made it relatively easy for her to pull her control back into place. But underneath, the agony remained. "I'm fine. Really."

Brady studied her, both puzzled and concerned. It was obvious that whatever had hurt her was now hidden beneath the ice of her shell, and she had command of herself again.

But there was something terribly wrong.

She'd never felt her loss so keenly before, Marissa thought, clasping her hands in front of her and gazing blindly toward the stage. She'd never known the desolation she felt in this moment. It made her feel brittle, as if she'd break into pieces at a touch. She wanted to find a dark corner, curl up, and let the hurt take her.

But she was surrounded by people. Brady was beside her. So the pain built without an outlet.

She'd never grieved, she realized; she'd taken up her life with utter authority and gone on as if nothing had happened, burying the aching torment. Now, bewildered, she realized the pain was rising inside her like a scream.

And the anger. Damn Kenneth for all the things he had taken away from her.

She felt Brady's worried gaze on her and couldn't summon the strength to reassure him. His look was a demand that irritated her already-frayed nerves, creating a rawness inside her.

He shouldn't even be here, she thought, deliberately and eagerly rechanneling her anger toward him, hoping it would push out the pain.

Why did the room seem so dim? Why was there so much noise? She jumped when someone across the table yelped in excitement.

"Congratulations, Paul and Kathy," Marissa heard Brady say. "I hope you'll enjoy the sculpture."

"You can be sure that we'll give it a good home," Paul said.

"We and our children will cherish it for years to come," Kathy said.

"Then I can consider the piece a success. Now if you'll excuse us, Marissa and I have to be going."

She felt him reach beneath her elbows and pull her to her feet. She heard people saying good-bye to her. "Good-bye," she murmured.

"Call me tomorrow," CeCe said.

"Tomorrow," she said.

Brady began guiding her through the tables toward the door. Her skin was so cold, he thought worriedly. What could have upset her so badly? Had he somehow pushed her too far?

Everyone wanted to talk to him. He spoke a word here and there, but he kept walking, making sure Marissa was with him every step of the way. He glowered with impatience while the young woman in the coatroom retrieved his denim jacket. He paid the valet triple his usual fee to make sure there would be no delay in getting the Jeep in front of the hotel.

All during the drive home, he kept an eye on her. Her body was stiff, her eyes were blank, her skin was paler than he had ever seen it.

At the house he took the keys from her nerveless fingers and opened the door. Wordlessly, she passed him and entered the house. He followed, tossing the jewelry case on the foyer table, and caught up with her in the living room.

With an instinctive need to comfort, he reached for her and pulled her into his arms. "Marissa, honey, what's wrong? Talk to me. What happened back there?"

He was trying to trap her, she thought, near the breaking point. She pushed against him. "No." His hold tightened, and she felt something begin to fracture in her.

"Just stay still," he said softly, soothingly. "Tell me how I can help you."

Tears spilled out of her eyes and down her cheeks. She struggled against him, beating his chest with her fists.

Fearing she would harm herself, he released her. But he stayed close. "You've got to calm down, Marissa. You're going to hurt yourself."

"Hurt? You don't know anything about hurt, especially mine."

"Then tell me."

She wiped the tears from her face, frantically searching her mind for a way to make him understand. "I've told you how you can help me, but you won't listen. I need you to *leave*. Haven't I told you that over and over?"

"Yes, you have."

"Then for God's sake, go!"

He held out his hands to her, but he didn't attempt to touch her. "Marissa, you were injured when you came into my life. I helped you heal, and I got in deeper with you than I ever imagined. But I became confused by the change in you when you regained your memory. Now I understand. You had a wound I couldn't see, and it's tearing you apart. Maybe I can heal that wound too."

"You can't."

"At least let me try."

"No!" Her short laugh held a hint of hysteria. "The best thing you can do for me is leave. Can't I make you see that?"

He exhaled slowly. "If I believed you, maybe I'd do as you say. But then again, if push came to shove, I don't know if I would or not. I've become real thick-headed where you're concerned. Haven't you figured it out yet?"

"Figured out what?"

"I love you." He silently swore. He hadn't meant

to say it so baldly, but in the emotionalism of the moment it had just come out. All he could do now was wait and see what effect his admission had on her.

She stilled, her body taut as she absorbed the shock waves of this new demand. "No! I won't *let* you love me. I won't *trust* you to love me."

He rubbed his hands over his eyes. "You want to explain that to me?"

"It's impossible to fight you," she said with a wild kind of anger, fighting anyway with everything that was in her. "So, all right, I'll tell you what you want to know, and then you'll understand, and then finally you'll leave me alone. I told you I'd been married before. Remember?"

He saw the pain beneath the anger and felt an anger of his own. "I'm not likely to forget the mention of another man in your life," he said more sharply than he had intended, "even if he was in your past."

She nodded, the heated emotion in his voice washing over her without touching her. "His name was Kenneth Wrightman. He was attractive, even sexy. He had a good personality and made me laugh. I saw him as everything I'd ever wanted and fell head over heels in love with him." She began to pace. The sheer silk crepe train trailed behind her. "Did I tell you my parents liked him?"

As his gaze followed her, his body tensed, braced for a blow. "You told me."

She laughed, a high-pitched sound that hurt him. "I saw that as one more endorsement. What I forgot was that my father had been unfaithful to my mother for years. I knew what to look for, but I couldn't see it. I was blind."

"Are you saying your husband saw other women?"

His question came to her as a discordant sound. "I knew what to look for, but I couldn't see it." She repeated the words as if she were talking to herself. "That was the irony. Kenneth began drinking. He tried first one job and then another, never succeeding. People began dropping hints to me about how they'd seen him out with other women. Money disappeared. I tried everything I knew, but I couldn't seem to make him happy. At last I considered divorce."

She stopped and rubbed her arms, suddenly cold. "But I found out I was pregnant."

As if he felt her chill, his blood froze.

"The baby threw a new light on everything. It became important to me to try to hold the marriage together. Unfortunately he didn't feel the same way. We were driving somewhere together, I've never been able to remember where. I didn't realize until I got into the car that he'd had too much to drink. I asked him to stop, to let me drive. We got into an argument. There was this terrific crash."

The stemmed tears began to flow again, running down her pale cheeks in hot crystal streams. "The car crumpled around me and I was trapped. I begged him to help me. He didn't even look at me. He simply got out of the car and walked away. I miscarried on the way to the hospital."

Her legs gave way and she sank into the nearest chair.

Brady let out a stream of curses. "I hope they hanged the bastard."

Her head dropped back onto the rolled rim of the chair and she looked at him through narrowed, misted eyes. "Turned out the accident wasn't his fault. It seems the man in the other car ran a red light. But it was all right. My lawyers came in and took over, and I never had to see Kenneth again."

Now he knew what he was up against, and for the very first time in his life, he could sense defeat closing in on him. He walked over to her. "What you went through is beyond words, Marissa. I understand why you wouldn't want to risk love again. But I'm not your ex-husband." Even to his ears, it sounded lame. "What I mean is—"

She shook her head wearily. "Stop trying, Brady. It's no good. I lost too much that night."

"That was years ago. Your heart should have had time to heal."

"It healed. It grew over with scar tissue until it was all closed up."

"It didn't heal. It just closed up. The pain is still there. That's why you're fighting so hard, but you fell in love with me when you were in Arkansas."

"Remembering why I couldn't trust my judgment took care of any love I might have felt for you."

He leaned down and placed his hands on the armrests of the chair. "You made a mistake, and you paid a price, and because of it, you can't let yourself believe that I won't hurt you. That's ridiculous."

She pushed him away with a violent shove and jerked to her feet. "You're simplifying the matter. I thought you said you understood."

"I do."

She held up a shaking finger. "For your own good, listen to me. There's a bond of trust between people who love each other. I saw it tonight between Paul and Kathy. Now, I have every reason to believe that you're a good man, but my lack of insight into a man once had tragic results. And, Brady, I'm sorry, but I just can't trust myself to trust you."

"You did in Arkansas. That proves that you have the capacity. You've just got to stop letting what happened to you stand in the way."

"But don't you see?" she asked quietly. "That's what I've been trying to say. I can't do that. I won't."

His shoulders slumped. "Is it really so futile?" His tone begged her to tell him no. "Have I really lost you?"

A deep, throbbing ache invaded her heart. "You never had me, Brady. Not really."

He nodded heavily and took a few steps away. He'd believed so fiercely that he could change her mind. Now he only felt empty, drained.

She stared at him, knew she had done the right thing, and wondered why the ache intensified with every beat of her heart.

The phone rang. It rang four times before it occurred to her to answer it. She crossed the room and picked up the receiver. "Hello."

"This is Sergeant Bill Robbins of the Dallas Police Department. I'm calling for Marissa Berryman."

"This is she."

"Ma'am, Cecilia Kavanaugh has been in an accident and has been taken to the hospital. We found your name and number in her purse. Are you a relative?"

Marissa froze. "CeCe? How is she?"

"She's unconscious, ma'am. The doctors at the hospital will be able to tell you more. Does she have a next of kin I can contact?"

She put her hand to her forehead, fighting off dizziness, conscious with some distant part of her mind that Brady had come to stand beside her. "Her parents are in Europe, but I'll be there right away."

She dropped the receiver into its cradle. "I've got to go to the hospital."

"I heard. I'll take you."

"I can drive myself," she said automatically.

"I'm sure you can, but you don't have to."

Eleven

The impersonality of the hospital strengthened and became part of the nightmarelike feeling that surrounded Marissa. Everything was antiseptically clean, sterile, and placed for efficiency. It seemed only the covers on the well-read magazines provided any real color. It was remarkably like her house, she thought dully.

"Marissa," Brady murmured.

"What?"

"The nurse just asked you a question."

"I—I'm sorry."

The nurse smiled with understanding. "I just asked if you could give us any medical history on Cecilia Kavanaugh."

"I know some of it." She rubbed at her brow, trying to think. "We had the chicken pox together when we were six. She caught the mumps from me when we were seven. She hasn't had any serious illnesses since, I'm sure. Nothing was wrong with her. She was perfectly fine when I saw her tonight. . . ." She felt Brady's hand on her shoulder.

"Do you know of any allergies she might have?" the nurse asked.

"No, none. She's always been so healthy. Please, can't you tell me anything about CeCe's condition?"

"I don't really know anything, but a doctor will be out in a moment."

Brady squeezed Marissa's shoulder. "We'll be in the waiting room," he said to the nurse. "Make sure the doctor finds us."

He guided her to a seat on a brown leather sofa and settled himself beside her.

"I don't understand," Marissa murmured. "Why CeCe? She's never hurt a soul in her life."

"She's going to be all right. You just have to keep telling yourself that."

"But what could have happened? We saw her only an hour or so ago. She'd had at most a glass of wine. And she was always such a careful driver."

"We can't always control what happens to us, Marissa. You should know that."

A white-coated doctor with serious brown eyes and a tired face walked around the corner. "Ms. Berryman?"

She jumped to her feet. "Yes. How's CeCe? How's Cecilia Kavanaugh?"

"She's still unconscious. However, she's been to radiology, and we're treating her for shock. The surgeon on call has been contacted, and he's on his way in."

She swayed and found Brady's hard body supporting her. "Surgeon? Why?"

"Ms. Berryman, your friend is in critical condition at the moment. She has extensive internal injuries and bleeding."

"But you can repair the damage, can't you? And stop the bleeding? She's going to be all right, isn't she?"

He seemed to hesitate. "Does she have any family, Ms. Berryman?"

"I've already told the nurse that her parents are in Europe."

"Do you know how to reach them?"

"I could call their maid if necessary. I'm sure she has their itinerary."

"Then I suggest you call her."

She stared at the doctor, horrified, and felt Brady take her hand. "My Lord, is it that bad?"

He considered her gravely. "I feel it would be best if her family could get here as soon as possible. Now if you'll excuse me, I have to scrub."

Brady's voice temporarily halted the doctor. "You will come and tell us as soon as you know anything, won't you?"

The doctor gave a nod and disappeared back around the corner.

Numb, Marissa glanced around. "Where's my purse? I have to call the Kavanaughs' home."

"You didn't bring your purse. I've got some change, and you can use my credit card to place the overseas call."

The next few hours passed in a haze. She reached the Kavanaughs' hotel in Paris and left a message. As soon as they received it, she knew they'd catch the first plane home, the Concorde if possible. They were caring people. Just like CeCe.

Perched on the edge of the couch, her body bent forward, her arms on her knees, she thought of CeCe lying on an operating table, her life in the balance. "She was always so full of life," she murmured, her eyes filling. "She had a tree house that we used to play in for hours. Sometimes we'd make a batch of fudge and take it up there. We'd laugh and eat until we were sick."

Brady held a Styrofoam coffee cup to her lips. "Take a drink."

She took a swallow of the sweetened coffee. "She's so alone in there."

"No she's not. You're here."

"But she doesn't know it. It's awful to be alone." *It seemed like she'd been alone forever.*

"Take a bite of this Danish," he said, holding the pastry in front of her.

She took a bite and sat back against the couch. Beside her, Brady did the same. "I don't think I told you that she asked me to ride with her to the benefit. She wanted me to go early and help with the auction. I was too caught up in my own problems and I said no. Maybe if I'd been with her . . ."

"The only difference that would have made is you would be in a second operating room right at this moment," he said quietly. "It wouldn't have helped her at all."

"But maybe—"

"Don't dwell on it. Just think of the good times." He raised his arm and put it around her. "Tell me some of the pranks you two used to play."

"Well . . ." She laid her head on his shoulder, shut her eyes, and thought of the time they'd double-dated and tried to convince their dates that they were twins. It had been fun, and she tried to recall why they'd done it. It seemed inspired at the time.

She drifted off and when she woke up, dawn was coming through the windows, and Brady was still holding her. Carefully she moved her head so that she could see his face. His eyes were closed, his breathing deep and even. His arms had to be cramped, she thought, yet he had held her for hours.

She'd been in a daze throughout the night. Most of the time she hadn't even been conscious that he'd been there with her. He hadn't said much; as she recalled she'd done a great deal of the talking. He'd fed her and given her coffee. He'd been concerned, he'd been kind, he'd shown her love.

Thanks to him, she hadn't been alone.

She shut her eyes as certain truths began to strike her. She remembered two men and two storms. One man had walked away from her, one man had saved her.

"Ms. Berryman?"

Her eyes flew open and she leaped to her feet. "Doctor, how is she?" She reached for Brady's hand; he was instantly beside her.

"From all appearances, Cecilia came through

the surgery well. We feel we have reason to be guardedly optimistic."

She sagged against Brady with relief. "Thank God."

"I suggest you go home and get some rest. Come back this evening. By then Cecilia should be awake."

Tears spilled out of her eyes before she could blink them away. "Thank you, Doctor. Thank you so much."

She turned to the man who had so quietly been her strength all night. "Brady, take me home, please."

Standing in the foyer of her house, still dressed in her long red dress, Marissa peered at Brady through a dense fringe of dark lashes. He appeared uncomfortable, and remembering the raw state they'd both been in before they'd received the call, she could understand his feeling ill at ease now that the crisis was over. He probably hoped to leave her as soon as possible, go back to the hotel and collect his things, and then head for Arkansas.

Had she finally succeeded in destroying his love for her? Dear Lord, she hoped not.

She clasped her hands loosely in front of her, glanced down at them, then looked back up at him. "I want to thank you for being with me last night."

"I'm just glad CeCe's going to come through all right."

She bit her bottom lip. He seemed so remote,

as if he were already back in Arkansas. "Are you hungry? I could rouse Lillian and have her make us breakfast." He shook his head. Her heart sank, but determinedly she tried again. "I have an idea. Maybe I could attempt waffles. With you here to give advice, I'm bound to do a better job."

Surprised, Brady considered her invitation, especially the mention of waffles, which inadvertently brought back memories of a sweeter time that had no place in the present.

Last night had been the worst night of his life. He'd tried so hard to get through to her and had failed completely. He'd taken her to the hospital, though he was sure she would have rather gone alone. He'd stayed with her, when half the time he was certain she didn't even know he was there. She'd nailed herself into a box where no one could get at her, and at the moment he didn't know if there was a way to get her out. He felt the best thing—actually the only thing—he could do was to drive back to Arkansas, rest, regain his perspective, perhaps even work . . . and then see.

But why was she asking him to breakfast? It had to be out of courtesy. Suddenly he found himself at the end of his rope, and he exploded with anger. "Save your civility for your society friends, Marissa. You don't have to play hostess to me out of a sense of duty. Too much has passed between us for that."

"I really want you to stay," she said, distressed that he had misinterpreted her intention.

His mouth twisted cynically. "Thanks, but no

thanks. The sooner I get on the road the better."
He made an attempt at a laugh. "Rodin probably
won't recognize me. I've been gone so long."

Alarm gripped her. She had to think of something to keep him from going. But what? "Brady,
wait. I—I need you to do something for me."

He eyed her cautiously. "What?"

"I . . ." Her mind raced. She'd hurt him so
badly. He needed more than words. This time
she had to be the one to give. "I need you to
unfasten my dress. And then I need you to
make love to me."

He stilled, but his heart slammed against his
ribs. "No, Marissa. Don't do this."

She stared at him a moment, the idea of
defeat ripping at her insides. The mist had
finally parted in her mind so that she could see
clearly, but she had to convince him of what
she was seeing. And she knew of only one way
to give him absolute assurance.

She went to him and laid trembling hands on
his chest. "I know I'm asking a lot."

"Yes, you are," he said raggedly. His face was
set in a harsh unyielding expression, but his
eyes revealed a torment. "*Why* are you asking
it?"

"You'll know if you make love to me."

"I don't need your damn pity, Marissa. I don't
want it."

She stood on tiptoe and pressed her lips to
his, her longing apparent as she strained against
him. "Does this feel like pity?"

Sensations threatened. He took her arms and
tried to push her away, but she linked her hands

behind his neck. "Dammit, Marissa. You nearly lost your best friend. That would shake anyone up. What you're experiencing now is a natural reaction. You were forced to consider death last night and you want a taste of life. But my nerves can't stand the therapy you think you want. You need sleep, and I need to leave."

"I know what I need, and it's you." She kissed him again, managing to insinuate her tongue between his hard lips and into the depths of his mouth. She couldn't believe her brazenness, but she was risking everything, and she prayed fervently it would work.

The response of his body was unmistakable. He'd hardened the minute she pressed against him. To allow his control to slip any further would be madness. "Stop this now before we won't be able to stop."

"Every time we kiss I think it couldn't get better, and then the next time it does."

Each word sent puffs of her hot sweet breath into his mouth, transmitting heat throughout him. The most glorious woman in the world was pressing her soft, warm body against him, telling him she wanted him. He groaned, surrender closer than was good for either of them.

"Trust me," she whispered. "I'll try to make sure you don't regret it."

He closed his eyes against the emotions that were searing him. The opportunity to have her one last time was too much for him. He'd make sense of this later, he decided, just as his mind snapped. He swept her into his arms and carried her into her bedroom. On the bed there he took off the beautiful red silk crepe sheath and found something even more beautiful—skin that begged to be caressed, curves that enticed, hollows that invited.

But he was in a hurry, frantically hungry for her. He wanted to indulge to excess the appetite of his senses, so that he would be full to bursting with her on the long, lonely road back to Arkansas.

She slowed him down. One by one, she undid the buttons of his shirt. Then she rasped the tips of her fingernails across the washboard muscles of his abdomen and used the pad of a finger to lightly trace the soft aureoles of his nipples.

His hands drove through her hair to clasp her head, dragging her mouth back to his. But she refused to be hurried. She broke free of his hold and slowly kissed her way through the dark curly hair that grew on his chest, up to the strong column of his neck and his jaw.

"What are you doing, Marissa?" His voice was a hoarse, barely recognizable growl. "Is this a new form of torture?"

"I don't know," she said, kissing the corner of his mouth, and at the same time unfastening his jeans. "Do you like it?"

A harsh breath tore from his lungs. "God, yes."

"Then it isn't torture." She slid her hands beneath his jeans until she could wrap her hand around him. The tenderness she used was exquisite. The finesse she used was mind-blowing. In some small corner of his mind, he remembered how in Arkansas he had taught her to caress him during their lovemaking. Blood beat heavily through his body until he thought he would explode. She had learned well.

"I can't take this anymore," he muttered, and hastily, jerkily skimmed off his jeans and his briefs.

She sat up, and one by one plucked the pins from her hair until the dark length was free of its coil and it fell in an azure-black cloud around her head and shoulders. When he was naked, she lay down on top of him. "There's always been something primitive about the way we make love," she murmured, sliding her velvet body slowly back and forth on him. "I never knew such feelings were possible for me."

Her breasts pressed against him, the stiffly pointing nipples grazed him, and her smoothness against his roughness created a friction and ignited a fire in him that he knew could no longer be controlled. A fierce need gripped his entire body; his resistance was over. He gathered her to him with arms that trembled and a passion that frightened him with its intensity. "'Marissa, I have to have you."

She raised up and brought herself down onto him. "You have me," she whispered.

He rolled over with her and plunged as deep as possible into her.

And she responded as if she'd looked into his mind, seen what he was feeling, and knew exactly what he needed. Her reaction went beyond passionate. Her every move anticipated then fulfilled his urgent demands. Little noises came from her throat that made him wild, and she did things with her mouth that made him even wilder. Then she quivered and tightened around him until he thought he would explode.

She was his every wish, and he was flooded with love and wonder. It was then that the realization came to him, suddenly, like a shooting star lighting up the night sky—she was making *love* to him. He couldn't hold back any longer.

They lay side by side, spent. His body had never been so completely satisfied, but his mind was working again, and the fear that he might have been wrong to think that she loved him kept him from looking at her. After what they'd just shared, he wasn't certain he'd be able to stand it if she rejected him now. He reached between them and curled his fingers around her hand. "Marissa, do you love me?"

"You aren't sure?" she asked, hesitant. "I was hoping you'd be able to tell."

His pulse surged, as a glimmer of hope appeared. "The way you made love to me was incredible, but . . ."

She laughed lightly and came up on her elbow so that she could see his face—so hard, so beloved. "I was inspired by you."

He gazed up at her. If he let himself, he could read so much into the tender loving expression he thought he saw in her amethyst eyes. But he refused to let the glimmer of hope become a blaze. "What happened?" he asked quietly.

She skimmed her fingers through the dark hair on his chest until her palm came to rest over his heart. "Things have been so complicated between us, but in the end it's come down to a very simple explanation. You were demanding a future with me, and I wasn't through with the past. Last night we pushed each other to the wall, but what we went through at the hospital cut through it all. You were there for me, and I was finally able to admit to myself that I need you very much."

"Are you saying that you can trust yourself and me?"

His continued uncertainty tore at her. She gently ran her hand across his broad chest. "My reaction in Arkansas when I first opened my eyes and saw you was a true one. I trust you implicitly. And as for trusting myself, I know now that it was never a question of judgment, but of knowledge. I didn't know Kenneth, and judgment fails when knowledge is absent. I didn't have a clear understanding of him, but I know you inside and out. You've never failed me, nor will you ever. And I'm going to try very hard to make sure that I never fail you either. That is, if you still want me."

He pulled her on top of him and tenderly cradled her face. "You can't begin to imagine how much I want you by my side for the rest of my life." He laughed and she felt the vibration of his joy inside her. "I love you with my entire being, Marissa."

She felt as if a heavy burden had just been lifted from her. "And I love you, so much. I'm amazed when I think about it. You and I fell in love the only way we could have. I fell in love with you because I couldn't remember why I shouldn't."

He smiled with understanding. "And I fell in love with you because you were helpless and vulnerable, and I was forced to open up a part of myself to help you. Once I'd done that, I couldn't close myself up again. And I didn't want to. You changed my life."

"You saved mine."

A shudder rippled through his lean body, and their lips joined in a kiss that was long, languid, deep, and spoke of the new security they felt about their future and each other.

"I want to be married on top of the mountain at sunrise," she whispered.

"Yes. That's what we'll do. Let's go home. Rodin will be waiting for us."

Tears of happiness clung to her lashes. "Thank God, I found you, Brady McCulloch."

THE EDITOR'S CORNER

There is never a dull moment in our LOVESWEPT offices where we're forever discussing new ideas for the line. So, fair warning, get ready for the fruits of two of our brainstorms . . . which, of course, we hope you will love.

First, expect a fabulous *visual* surprise next month. We are going to reflect the brilliance of our LOVESWEPT author's romances by adding *shimmer* to our covers. Our gorgeous new look features metallic ink frames around our cover illustrations. We've also had a calligrapher devote his talent to reworking the LOVESWEPT lettering into a lacy script and it will be embossed in white on the top metallic border of the books. Each month has a color of its own. (Look for gleaming blue next month . . . for glimmering rosy red the following month.) So what will set apart the books in a given month? Well, the author's name, the book's title, and a tiny decorative border around the art panel will have its own special color. Just beautiful. We've worked long and hard on our new look, and we're popping with prideful enthusiasm for it. Special thanks go to our creative and tireless art director, Marva Martin.

Around here we believe that resting on laurels must be boring (could it also be painful?). And, like most women, all of us LOVESWEPT ladies, authors and editors, are out to prove something as time goes by—namely, *the older we get . . . the better we get . . . in every way!*

Our exciting news has taken so much space that I'm afraid I can give only brief descriptions of the wonderful romances we have coming your way next month. However, I'm sure that just the names of the authors will whet your appetite for the terrific love stories we have in our bright new packages.

Delightful Kay Hooper has come up with a real treat—not just one, but many—the first of which you'll get to sample next month. Kay is writing a number of LOVE-SWEPTs that are based on fairy tales . . . but bringing

(continued)

their themes completely (and excitingly!) up to date. Next month, *Once Upon a Time* ... **GOLDEN THREADS,** LOVESWEPT #348, tells the love story of Lara Mason who, like Rapunzel, was isolated in a lonely, alien life ... until Devon Shane came along to help her solve the problems that had driven her into hiding. An absolutely unforgettable romance!

In a book that's as much snappy fun as its title, Doris Parmett gives us **SASSY,** LOVESWEPT #349. Supermodel Sassy Shaw thought she was headed for a peaceful vacation in Nevada, but rancher Luke Cassidy had other plans for his gorgeous guest. This is a real sizzler ... with lots of guffaws thrown in. We think you'll love it.

The thrilling conclusion of The Cherokee Trilogy arrives from Deborah Smith next month with **KAT'S TALE,** LOVESWEPT #350. Kat Gallatin, whom you've met briefly in the first two of the Cherokee books, is unorthodox ... to say the least. She's also adorable and heartwarming, a real heroine. That's what Nathan Chatham thinks, too, as he gets involved with the wildcat he wants to see turn kitten in his arms. A fabulous conclusion to this wonderful trio of books—a must read!

Tami Hoag tugs at your heart in **STRAIGHT FROM THE HEART,** LOVESWEPT #351. Jace Cooper, an injured baseball star, was back in town, and Rebecca Bradshaw was desperate to avoid him—an impossibility since she was assigned to be his physical therapist. In this sizzler Rebecca and Jace have to work out the problems of a wild past full of misunderstanding. **STRAIGHT FROM THE HEART** is a sensual and emotional delight from talented Tami.

Patt Bucheister gives us another real charmer in **ELU-SIVE GYPSY,** LOVESWEPT #352. Rachel Hyatt is a Justice of the Peace who married Thorn Canon's aunt to some stranger ... and he's furious when he first encounters her. But not for long. She makes his blood boil (not his temper) and thoroughly enchants him with her

(continued)

off-beat way of looking at the world. Don't miss this marvelous love story!

THE WITCHING TIME, LOVESWEPT #353, by Fayrene Preston is delicious, a true dessert of a romance, so we saved it for the end of LOVESWEPT's September feast. Something strange was going on in Hilary, Virginia. Noah Braxton felt it the second he arrived in town. He knew it when he encountered a golden-haired, blue-eyed witch named Rhiannon York who cast a spell on him. With his quaint aunts, Rhiannon's extraordinary cat, and a mysterious secret in town, Noah finds his romance with the incredible Rhiannon gets unbelievably, but delightfully, complex. A true confection of a romance that you can relish, knowing it doesn't have a single calorie in it to add to your waistline.

We hope you will enjoy our present to you of our new look next month. We want you to be proud of being seen reading a LOVESWEPT in public, and we think you will be with these beautifully packaged romances. Our goal was to give you prettier and more discreet covers with a touch of elegance. Let us know if you think we succeeded.

With every good wish,

Carolyn Nichols

Carolyn Nichols
Editor
LOVESWEPT
Bantam Books
666 Fifth Avenue
New York, NY 10103

THE DELANEY DYNASTY

Men and women whose loves and passions are so glorious it takes many great romance novels by three bestselling authors to tell their tempestuous stories.

THE SHAMROCK TRINITY

- ☐ 21975 RAFE, THE MAVERICK
  by Kay Hooper $2.95
- ☐ 21976 YORK, THE RENEGADE
  by Iris Johansen $2.95
- ☐ 21977 BURKE, THE KINGPIN
  by Fayrene Preston $2.95

THE DELANEYS OF KILLAROO

- ☐ 21872 ADELAIDE, THE ENCHANTRESS
  by Kay Hooper $2.75
- ☐ 21873 MATILDA, THE ADVENTURESS
  by Iris Johansen $2.75
- ☐ 21874 SYDNEY, THE TEMPTRESS
  by Fayrene Preston $2.75

- ☐ 26991 THIS FIERCE SPLENDOR
  by Iris Johansen $3.95

Now Available!
THE DELANEYS: *The Untamed Years*

- ☐ 21897 GOLDEN FLAMES *by Kay Hooper* $3.50
- ☐ 21898 WILD SILVER *by Iris Johansen* $3.50
- ☐ 21999 COPPER FIRE *by Fayrene Preston* $3.50

Buy these books at your local bookstore or use this page to order.

Prices and availability subject to change without notice.

- -

Bantam Books, Dept. SW7, 414 East Golf Road, Des Plaines, IL 60016

Please send me the books I have checked above. I am enclosing $_____ (please add $2.00 to cover postage and handling). Send check or money order—no cash or C.O.D.s please.

Mr/Ms _____

Address _____

City/State _____ Zip _____

SW7—4/89

Please allow four to six weeks for delivery. This offer expires 10/89.

Special Offer
Buy a Bantam Book
for only 50¢.

Now you can have Bantam's catalog filled with hundreds of titles plus take advantage of our unique and exciting bonus book offer. A special offer which gives you the opportunity to purchase a Bantam book for only 50¢. Here's how!

By ordering any five books at the regular price per order, you can also choose any other single book listed (up to a $5.95 value) for just 50¢. Some restrictions do apply, but for further details why not send for Bantam's catalog of titles today!

Just send us your name and address and we will send you a catalog!